LORI·ANNE·COHEN
MARKED
BY THE
VAMPIRE

Dedicated to my people on the Romance Riot Discord.
Thank you for the love, support and the laughs.

Some things to know before you read!

Please see list below before you read.

- Violence

- Swearing

- Prison

- Discussion of Parental Death

- Explicit Sexual Situations

  - Includes: anal sex

- Kink

  - Includes: biting/marking

If you come across others, please email me at lacohenwrites@gmail.com. I have endeavored to include them all, but I realize I may have missed some.

This book
is a work of fiction. Any resemblance to people, places or events is entirely
coincidental.

Copyright
2023 ©Lori-Anne Cohen

NO AI TRAINING ALLOWED
This author does not approve the use of her work for any AI training.

All rights reserved. No part of this book may be reproduced or used
in any manner without the prior written permission of the copyright owner,
except for the use of brief quotations in a book review.

Paperback: 978-1-7370838-7-0
E-book: 978-1-7370838-6-3

Editor: Kyleigh Poultney
Cover: GetCovers

Printed
by Kindle Direct Publishing in the USA

<h1 style="text-align: center; font-family: cursive;">ABIGAIL</h1>

The thing is, when you walk past him, you need to make yourself as unobtrusive as possible. I wear an oversized trench coat when I can, always look down, and hurry past. You do not want to catch his attention. Two old ladies did once, and now they never pass without him saying something. And they, of course, always say something back. I am not sure why he thinks it's amusing to be out there during the morning and evening commutes while people rush past.

He's sired by one of the most powerful vampires in the world and acts accordingly. He can trace his lineage back to one of the original vampire lines, and seems to play at being a businessman, though he has never been involved in any company I've worked for. He owns the restaurant I pass every morning on my way to work. It's only been open for a matter of months, and it's all anyone can talk about. It feels odd for him to spend so much time here. I can't figure it out.

He's dangerous. But he's also fucking gorgeous, if I am being honest. Well over six feet tall with dark hair and dark eyes that sometimes flash amber. I have no idea how old he is, though I suspect he is quite old. A menace emanates from him that feels almost ancient. He's originally from Korea. That much is a matter of public record. His forearms are fully tattooed, and I've idly wondered if the rest of him is tattooed.

Okay, not so idly. I did say he was gorgeous, and I have a real weakness for men with tattoos.

I've managed to perfect looking at him while keeping my head down. I'd be lying if I said he hadn't starred in my late-night fantasies, but I am still not engaging.

Because when I say he's dangerous, it has a double meaning. Yes, he's the expected kind of dangerous a powerful vampire would be. It's alluring, which makes him personally dangerous for me. He's my catnip. I could change my path to work, but I don't. I am afraid of him noticing me, but I also need to see him. Although, if he did notice, nothing would come of it.

Once, when I passed by on my way home from work, he was speaking with a tall, gorgeous brunette—another vampire. You can always tell. It doesn't surprise me that he goes for the leggy model type. I am very comfortable with myself, at five foot six with some nice curves, but weight around my middle. I like my curves a lot, but I would never be mistaken for a model.

I walked by quickly tonight, trying not to take another peek at him. And once again, I ignored the disappointment sitting in my chest when he didn't notice me. Silly, I know. It's been too long since I've been with anyone. Maybe I'd fix that tonight. I was going out with a few friends who lived uptown. I'd need to pass this way, but I didn't think I'd need to worry about seeing him a third time.

This is why it was a total surprise to me when, two hours later, my arm was grabbed as I hurried past, clutching my trench coat closed. "Well, little flower," a deep and troublingly recognizable voice asked, "Where are we going in such a hurry?"

Oh fuck.

I looked up at him. "Me?" My voice was only a little shaky. I didn't even stammer. His grip was firm, but I could pull away if I wanted to. Why wasn't I?

"Yes, you. You walk by twice a day during the week, but never in the evenings and never on weekends. So, where are you in such a hurry to get to?" My eyes widened in surprise. He'd noticed me? I struggled to wrap my head around that little nugget of information. He didn't wait for me to answer, pulling me closer. "I think you and I should have a drink, before I let you go off into the night."

"A drink?" I was shocked. What was happening here? "No, I'm meeting friends. I don't have time for a ... drink." In truth, I was early because I always was. I didn't like to hurry, so I padded my time by about thirty to forty minutes.

"Oh, I am sure you do," he replied silkily. "Come, now."

"I'm not sure I can afford this," I replied, frowning.

"I own this establishment. I wouldn't worry about that."

"That's not what I meant," I muttered, but I followed him. "I have thirty minutes before I need to be on my way."

"Of course." He led me inside and stopped at the bar quickly to say something to the bartender. Then he led me to a cozy booth at the back of the restaurant. I went to sit, and he stopped me.

"Hold a moment," he said. He came up behind me and gently peeled back my trench, pulling it off me. "Let's remove this, shall we?" I couldn't be absolutely sure, but I could have sworn his hand trailed down my back. I shivered at the thought.

His gaze roamed over my body. He smiled. I wore a silver sequined skirt hitting above my knee and a soft short-sleeved white sweater with a scoop neck. The outfit showed off my hourglass figure well.

"I suspected you might be spectacular under all that coat."

"Thank you?" I am unsure what was happening here because he couldn't think I was any kind of beauty. I am not even sure why I followed him. Curiosity? Lust? I'm an idiot? I slid into the booth, and he slid in on the other side.

I looked around. "You like to survey your kingdom, I see." I cringed at my words, but he laughed.

"I do, yes." His arm snaked out along the banquette behind me. His hand was close to my shoulder. It was very distracting. "Do you like it?"

"I do. It's reminiscent of a speakeasy."

"Delightful. That was the intention."

A waiter approached us, opened a bottle of white wine, and poured two glasses. I picked my glass up, took a sip, and smiled. "Oh, this is lovely! It's so buttery."

"I am glad you like it. It's one of mine."

"Pardon?"

"I own a winery."

"Naturally," I replied. I should be a lot more nervous, but this whole thing was so surreal like I was having an out-of-body experience. He smelled amazing—dangerous, and danger apparently smells divine.

"I have been remiss, though. I haven't asked your name."

He was serving me exceptional wine; I suppose I could tell him my name. "Abigail Eastman."

"What a lovely old-fashioned name."

I narrowed my eyes, wondering if he was mocking me, but his tone seemed sincere. "Thank you." I took another sip of wine. "So, why am I here?"

"Why are any of us here, Abigail?" He lifted my free hand. His touch made me feel ... well, like climbing into his lap and staying there. I really did need to get laid.

"You know what I mean, Anderson." I wanted to show him I knew who he was. I wondered what name he was born with, because I knew it wasn't the one he was using. When you've been alive for so long, you would pick up and discard names like it means nothing. But what does it do to someone to constantly reinvent themselves?

"Oh, you know my name. I'm flattered. You're here because I wanted you here."

"But why?" I couldn't figure out if he was completely insufferable or just hot. It was probably both. No, it was definitely both.

"I wanted to see what color your eyes were. Your head is always down when you pass me."

"I am surprised you noticed me."

"I noticed your scent."

I took the last sip of wine and shook my head. "I don't know how to respond to that." I really wasn't ready to know anything about how I smelled to a vampire.

He poured me another glass of wine and stared at me. I felt like I was caught in a trap.

"You don't need to respond any particular way. Just enjoy your wine."

I sipped my wine, as we sat in a surprisingly comfortable silence. Eventually, I looked at my watch. "I need to go. I don't like to be late."

"Of course. Whatever you wish."

He walked me to the door, my coat slung over his arm. I put my hand out, and he handed it back to me. "I hope never to see that coat again now that we're acquainted."

Had he figured out that I'd been using it to hide? Fucking great. "We'll see. Thank you for the wine. It was delicious."

He picked up my hand, flipped it over, and kissed the pulse point on my wrist. I tried hard not to melt on the spot. He lifted his head and pulled me closer. I must have looked startled as his next words were, "No need to look worried, little flower. I don't bite."

"I highly doubt that's true," I replied, a little too breathlessly for my own liking.

He laughed softly. "Oh, you've found me out. You're correct. I do bite. But not just to feed, sometimes to bring pleasure." He dropped my hand and all but glided back into the restaurant.

I stood for a moment, trying to get my libido under control. If there was ever a mic drop moment, that was it. He couldn't know what his words had done to me. I mentally snapped myself out of it. I took a deep breath and escaped to the relative safety of an uptown bar and my friends.

ANDERSON

She thought I hadn't noticed her. How wrong she was. I scented her the first day she walked by me a little over a year ago. She had been clutching that trench coat to her as if it could protect her from me. It never could. Especially now that I had her scent.

She'd often look and bite her tongue when those two old women and I sparred. She smelled so damned sweet—like honeyed lilacs. And that's why I never did anything about it. I am very much aware of how I am seen. I'm the villain, and women like her, who smell so sweet, are not for the likes of me.

But today, I could scent something spicy underneath the sweet. And that, I couldn't ignore. It pulled me to her. I had to stop her, if only to see her eyes for once. I was rewarded when she looked up, and I saw those cornflower blue eyes of hers. She looked a bit wary, but oddly I did not see or sense fear, although it would have been smart of her. But the lack of fear made me bold.

I picked up my phone and dialed Jack. "I need to find out where an Abigail Eastman lives. I suspect it's around the restaurant since she walks by every day. Five foot six, long brown hair, blue eyes, and probably about forty." I listened for a moment. "Jack, I don't pay you to make decisions about women for me. The address. Now, please."

I made my rounds, visited the tables, and checked the kitchen before Jack called me back with the information I wanted. He also managed to find out what she did for a living and where she worked. "The thing is, boss, she used to live uptown—a nice apartment overlooking the park."

"And she moved here to slum with us? Odd. Do we know why?"

"Does the name Jacob Eastman ring a bell?"

"It does. CFO for Allied Tech, right? Did something happen to him?"

"Yup. He went to jail. He was convicted of embezzlement. Under-reporting earnings and pocketing the difference. Abigail's father."

Interesting. "Was she involved?" Something about Jacob Eastman tickled the back of my head, but I couldn't say why.

"Not at all. She's clean, as far as I know. But she sold her apartment, his home, and everything in them to help make restitution. Then submitted to a thorough investigation at her own company to prove she was honest."

For some reason, that pissed me off. She'd done everything she could to try and make it right, and they still made her jump through hoops to keep her job. "Where does she work?"

"Power Dynamics. She's a senior VP of accounting. Though she also has a law degree. It must be said her team stuck by her. They willingly submitted to the investigation as well to help clear her."

"Find me something on the people who ran the investigation," I said.

"It was internal. The CFO and board members conducted it. The CEO was aware, but he didn't request it." Jack had gotten a lot of information in a short time. This was one reason he was my second in command.

Fucking witch hunts. "Fine. Find me something on all of them."

"Anderson, when did you meet this woman?"

"Officially, today. But I've seen her almost daily for over a year." She'd learned how to make herself small and invisible. I wasn't sure if that was really because of me, or because of everyone else's prying fucking eyes.

Jack sighed. "Anderson, she's human."

"And so are you. Your point?" I didn't quite understand why I was digging in so hard, but something was pulling me toward this woman, and I was willing to go along. At my age, you know when to trust your instincts and when not to. Now was the time to trust them.

"You don't get involved with human women."

"I'm not involved." *Yet.* "Jack, just do what I'm asking. Find me something I can use."

"You got it. I hope you know what you're doing."

I hung up. I always know what I'm doing. I was very much aware of that fact much later when I stood across the street from her apartment as a car pulled up. She got out on the passenger side. "Thanks for the ride, Peter. You and my girl get home safely, please!" There was a response from the car, and Abigail laughed. Her scent of lilacs wafted across to me. "No doubt! I'll see you tomorrow, Lacey!" The doorman held the door for her, and she thanked him, chatting for a moment.

I waited until the fourth-floor light came on. Jack had texted me her address and that her apartment faced the street. Not many buildings around here had a doorman, so she wasn't exactly suffering by living downtown. The blinds were closed, but the light offered me her silhouette. She removed her shoes, pulled her sweater off, and shimmied out of her skirt. I groaned inwardly at the raging hard-on I had suddenly.

Jack was right; I kept away from human women. Vampires understood each other, and in my case, it was just easier to be with my kind. Humans have known about us for at least two centuries and mostly have come to accept our presence. There had been years of bloodshed when the first vampire made himself known, but in time, humans had come to see that we were no worse than the other monsters that hid under their beds.

My vampire family had been the power behind many thrones, governments, and corporations for centuries. We didn't keep that position because we were sweethearts. Vampires becoming public knowledge had not changed that. On the contrary, in the end, it has made it easier for us to be honest in our business dealings.

I owned the restaurant because I enjoyed it and because it looked good. But mostly because I could keep tabs on things easily. Every single server, bartender, host, and hostess were my eyes and ears. It was one of the most exclusive restaurants in the city, for no other reason than because I owned it and because it was pricy. People associate exclusivity with money. That's a gross miscalculation on their part, though. It's an illusion. Power is also an illusion. And I was good at *illusion*. I was the best, in fact.

I considered dropping this whole thing with Abigail Eastman. She was good, and I didn't want to ruin that. Then I heard her laugh. And in that moment, I knew I would do whatever it took to have her.

I watch her peek through the blinds. She couldn't see me, I'm sure of that. But I wondered if she could sense me. A few minutes later, her light went out, and I walked home. I liked walking late at night. Most humans found it quiet, but the city was never completely silent. And I could hear all the sounds they couldn't.

Abigail was hesitant, and I could understand that. But I had spent the last year watching her clutch that ridiculous coat to her, and that time was over. Abigail was not a woman who should be hiding herself. I wanted her, and I wanted to know why she was hiding. I came up with a plan on the way back to the restaurant. My little flower was going to bloom if I had it my way.

<h1 style="text-align:center">ABIGAIL</h1>

"Okay, so he just grabbed your arm and cajoled you into having a drink? You?" Lacey and I were sitting on my couch at opposite ends, facing each other with our feet touching. We'd sat this way since we were kids, there was no reason to stop now. "I've seen what you can do, Abs. No one *makes* you do anything."

"I'm sorry, have you seen him?"

"I have, but you're never one to be turned by a pretty face."

"He's more than a pretty face. I don't know how to explain it. He was... electric. Yes, he's dangerous and completely out of my league, but I mean, I was caught." I *wanted* to be caught by him. I hadn't stopped thinking about him, though I am sure he had moved on right after I left. Bastard.

"First off, I don't care if he's sex on a stick, he is not out of your league. I'm surprised. But it explains why you were a little off last night."

"I was?"

"You were. But only I noticed." I should have known she'd sense that. "I've been worried about you since you moved downtown. And after that fucking joke of an investigation..."

"Lacey, come on now!"

"No, it was a joke. And this invisible act of yours? Girl! I know you!" I gave her a warning look, and she held up her hands in surrender, changing the subject. "Man, vampires are supposed to be dynamos in bed."

"I'm going to tell your husband you said that," I admonished.

"Oh please, Peter and I discuss it all the time. There's a gorgeous vampire couple in our building. We've chatted a few times, and they seemed, you know, interested."

I gaped at my oldest friend. "Lacey Monahan!"

"Peter and I like a little adventure in the bedroom, and this is nothing different."

I nodded. "Your mother would keel over if she knew you were going to swing with vampires."

"Good, maybe I'll tell the old bitch then. Send her some video of me getting railed by a vampire."

I laughed. "I almost want a video of that."

"I don't think you'll need it. You're going to have your own vampire."

I shook my head. "Don't be silly."

There was a knock at the apartment door, and I frowned. "Oh God, I hope this isn't a building thing." I liked this building because people kept to themselves. I went over to the door and looked through the peephole. On the other side was a tall, thin man. I thought he might be a vampire, but I couldn't be sure based on looks alone. "Can I help you?" I asked.

"Yes, Miss Eastman. Anderson Jeon sent me."

Lacey crept up behind me. "Prove it."

He sighed, and the man held up a bottle of the same wine I'd had last night. *I'll be damned*, I thought, opening the door. "Come in," I said.

He came in, carrying the crate with such ease, that I decided he was definitely a vampire. He set it down and handed me the bottle, which I immediately handed to Lacey. "Mr. Jeon has asked me to deliver a crate of the wine you shared last night and to ask you to dine with him tonight."

"Excuse me?" He wanted to have dinner with me?

"Dinner tonight, Miss. With Mr. Jeon."

I blinked at him. "I don't think..."

"She accepts," Lacey said.

"Lacey!"

"Hush, Abbie, you're going to dinner." She turned to the vampire in my living room. "Please tell Mr. Jeon that Miss Eastman would be delighted to dine with him tonight. She has no known food allergies, but her favorite foods are lobster and steak, and her favorite flowers are pink cabbage roses. She finds regular roses fussy."

The vampire cracked a smile. "I will certainly tell him all of that."

"Wonderful. And, of course, thank him for the wine."

"I swear to God, Lacey, I might kill you."

"No, you won't." Lacey smiled.

"Someone will be here to pick you up at seven p.m."

"I'd prefer to walk. It's not far. Shut up, Lacey," I said, pointing a finger at her.

"Fine, Miss. He thought you might feel that way. Your escorts will be downstairs at seven p.m. to walk you to the restaurant." He paused. "They'll be vampires."

"I do not need an escort."

"She'll take the escort," Lacey said. "Stop being stubborn."

I rolled my eyes. "Fine!"

The man bowed and left. Who even bows anymore?

Lacey was already in the kitchen opening the bottle. "The bottle is still cold! We're having some. Then we're going to pick out an outfit for tonight. Something that shows your shape off. Something that says, 'Fuck me!'"

"Lacey! For chrissakes!"

"I love you but shut up. He's obviously into you. You are most definitely into him. This is gonna be great!"

I rolled my eyes. "What am I going to do with a case of wine?" I groaned.

Lacey handed me a glass, and we clinked. She took a sip. "Fuck, this is good. For starters, I'm taking a couple of bottles home. Least I can do."

"He is going to eat me alive."

"Only if you're very lucky!"

***

At exactly seven p.m., I stepped outside to find two stoic-looking vampires waiting for me; a tall black woman with braids and a shorter guy who looked achingly young, his face still that of a boy's verging on manhood. I wondered how old he was when he'd been turned. They were wearing earpieces and dark sunglasses. I raised my eyebrows. "Are you the Men in Black come to take me away?"

The woman curled her lip. "Do I look like fucking Will Smith to you?"

"No, Tommy Lee Jones." This situation may be unfamiliar, but I wouldn't let these two see any nerves.

"Surely, Miss, I'm Will Smith in this scenario," the male vampire replied. "I'm Keith. This here is Soames. We're here to escort you to Mr. Jeon." His accent was pure Ireland.

I smiled at him; I couldn't help it. "I figured that."

Soames remained unsmiling but lifted her sunglasses. Her eyes were opaque, and I assumed Keith's were as well. "We don't like to shock the humans," she said, referencing the eyes.

"Ah," I replied. "Let's get going then."

I pivoted and walked, assuming they'd follow.

"You're not curious, are you?" Soames asked.

"You were doing it for shock value—to test me. Why give you what you want by asking questions?"

"She's got you there, Soames," Keith laughed.

I shrugged. "I already know why your eyes are like that. Vampires under one hundred years old have opaque eyes. No one is sure why any longer, a possible holdover from having to live in the dark eons ago. But you and your boss are not my first vampires."

Keith chuckled behind me, but Soames grunted. I kept walking and mostly ignored the two vampires behind me. I didn't need the escort, but I couldn't help but be amused by how chatty Keith was versus how taciturn Soames was. I suspected Keith of putting the Irish brogue on a bit thicker because he knew it irritated her.

Soon the restaurant came into view, along with Anderson. My heart may have stopped for a moment. He was dressed in black from head to toe; jacket, shirt, pants. He looked like some kind of dark God. The shirt was unbuttoned enough to reveal even more tattoos than usual, and I sent up a silent prayer of thanks for that. He leaned casually against the wall, watching me as I approached him. I slowed and put a little extra wiggle in my step. He smirked and raised one perfect eyebrow at me.

Someone chuckled behind me. "Well played, Miss Eastman." Soames sounded a little impressed.

"It's a good dress. I may as well use it to my advantage," I replied.

When I had almost reached him, he peeled himself off the wall and sauntered towards me. His eyes traveled up my body, then down, and my blood heated at the attention. I wore a deep blue knit dress that hugged my curves. Based on his look, he liked what he saw.

"Miss Eastman." He picked up my hand and laid his lips across my knuckles. "I am so pleased you were able to join me this evening."

Oh, we were playing it that way, huh? "Thank you for inviting me, Mr. Jeon. And thank you for the wine. A case was most generous."

"My pleasure," he purred. He eyed my escorts, and suddenly his voice was all business. "Well done, you two."

"Thank you, sir," Soames answered. Keith nodded his head.

"You two are due at warehouse A in thirty minutes. I suggest you make haste."

They nodded. "Right away, sir," Keith answered this time.

"Thank you both for the escort," I said.

"Most welcome, Miss Eastman." Keith smiled at me, and they were off.

I turned to Anderson. "I am quite capable of walking five blocks by myself. This is a decent neighborhood."

"I always safeguard precious items, Abigail."

"I see." Great comeback, Abbie. Really on your verbal game there.

He held the door open for me. "Shall we?" I nodded and made my way inside. He put his hand on my low back to guide me, and surprisingly we didn't head toward the back booth. We ascended a small flight of stairs and walked down a long hallway. He opened the door and ushered me inside. "I thought we'd dine privately this evening," he said.

I looked around. There was a table for two in the middle of the room. The centerpiece was a small vase of pink cabbage roses. At the opposite end of the room was a chaise longue by a fireplace, but there was no fire since it wasn't cold out.

I turned to him. "Quite the seduction scene," I remarked.

He licked his lips. "Anything worth doing is worth doing well." He approached the table and pulled the champagne out of the ice bucket. He opened it quickly and quietly, pouring me some.

"Thank you," I said, taking the glass. He clinked his to mine, and we drank. "What are we toasting to?"

"You in that dress," came the reply.

"Laying it on a bit thick there. How about a real answer?"

"Fine then, you *out* of that dress."

Despite myself, I laughed. He looked startled by this, which made me laugh harder. He came around the table, pulled me to him, and ghosted his lips over mine. It was barely a kiss, but every nerve ending in my body was at attention.

He pulled back but didn't let me go. "You are the damnedest woman," he said, rubbing his thumb along the seam of my lips before replacing it with his tongue. He took my bottom lip between his lips and sucked. I hadn't felt fangs, so they must retract. Then again, the lust pooling in my belly was making it hard to think clearly.

Despite what I had said to Soames and Keith, my dealings with vampires had been slim. Most of my information was second-hand—stuff I'd read or watched.

"Anderson," I said, "what if someone comes in?"

No one is coming in without knocking first." He pulled me closer, and I could feel his erection. I groaned softly, and he kissed me again, more aggressively. It was a demand, and I was helpless to do anything but give in. I opened my mouth so my tongue could mingle with his. He groaned this time.

Can you orgasm from a kiss?

He pulled back, and I frowned at him. He rubbed his thumb over my bottom lip and laughed softly. "I invited you for dinner. And dinner you shall have." He walked over to the door, pressed a small button, and then pulled my seat out for me.

"Thank you," I said, noticing his hands shaking a little. I was pleased to see that he was also flustered by our kiss. Maybe he had pulled back in order to assert some control over his own feelings.

"Most welcome." He poured more champagne and sat. A few moments later, there was a light knock. "Come in," he called.

Two servers came in and placed a small plate in front of each of us, a scallop starter. We made small talk until the entrees were brought in—lobster tails with a petite filet mignon. Once the servers left, I looked at him. "This is lovely, but I need to tell you my favorite meal is actually a cheeseburger and fries. I love both lobster and steak, but I will eat a burger any day of the week."

"Ah, your friend was testing me."

"She was. And now that we have our entrees, small talk is over. How did you find out where I lived?"

"Honestly, Abigail, that insults both of us. You know I am quite able find anyone's information easily."

"What else did you find out?" My eyes narrowed.

"I found out about your father if that's what you're alluding to."

"It is. So, you know why I moved then?" Anderson's people were good. However, a lot of it was a matter of public record. He nodded. I took a bite of steak and closed my eyes for a moment. "This is amazing. How come you weren't aware of it previously? I thought everything happening in this city was under your purview." The reasons I moved downtown weren't what I let most people believe they were. But that was my business.

"Hardly. Some corporations, yours and your father's, for instance, choose not to involve themselves with vampires. We respect that. Unless it becomes a problem."

His tone gave me pause. Were Allied Tech and Power Dynamics about to come under intense vampire scrutiny? We had just met, but I got the feeling Anderson didn't appreciate how things had gone down.

"When the issues with your father arose, I was out of the country, and my younger brother was minding the store. He is not as diligent in his responsibilities."

"How much younger is he than you?" I hoped this wasn't a rude question.

"Phillip is approximately a millennium younger than I am."

"He's a thousand years younger than you?" I was incredulous.

"Yes. I'm around twelve hundred years old. Give or take five years."

"Jesus! This is quite the age gap." I gestured to the both of us with my fork. Once again, my agile wit surfaces.

He smiled. "Does it bother you?"

"I don't think so. It's not like you look your age. Does it bother you?" It *was* odd, but I wasn't bothered ... I didn't think.

"I can't let it, so I don't. What else would you like to know?"

"You don't mind questions?" I'd finished my lobster tail, so I speared some steak as I frowned.

"I do not." He lifted a piece of lobster on his fork and then offered me the bite. Why was that hot? "Take it, Abigail." I took the bite, my heart beating faster at his commanding tone. A reaction he was not unaware of as he smiled at me wolfishly. *Fucker.*

I took a sip of champagne and cleared my throat. "Vampires need blood, but you also eat. And I've seen you in daylight. Could you always do both things?"

"Centuries ago, it was true we could only roam a night. But we've evolved since then. As such, we can be out in the daylight and eat. Newer vampires need to build up their tolerance for both." He ran a finger down his champagne flute, then took a sip. "Soames and Keith are examples of that. They are fine with daylight, and as they both enjoyed eating when they were mortal, they have worked to enjoy food once more. But they are of my line, so they are stronger than most their age. Not all vampires like to eat. I can take it or leave it. It helps when the company is superlative." He smiled at me.

I smiled at the compliment but moved on. "Interesting." I meant that. "What about sleep?"

"I don't need to sleep, really, but I do sometimes. And there are times when I need rest. I find the act of it comforting."

Before I could say anything else, there was another knock. The entrée was whisked away, and one chocolate mousse was set down, along with a bottle of brandy and two snifters.

"Is there anything else, Mr. Jeon?" The server asked.

"No, Andrew. Thank you. Please see to your other duties. No one is to bother us."

"Absolutely, sir."

Once they left, Anderson poured us some brandy. I took a sip and sighed contentedly. He took off his jacket and slowly rolled his sleeves. My mouth watered. Forearm porn is real; ask any woman, and his forearms were sexy as hell. And so very tattooed.

"Do you like what you see, Abigail?" He asked without looking away from his task.

"I do," I answered. I realized right then not only was I not afraid of him, but I was also comfortable with him. I hoped he was interested in me, and this wasn't about my father. I had had a lifetime of men trying to get close to me, thinking my father could do something for them. I had tried to date after he went to prison, but men liked the fact he was infamous and wanted to brag they'd fucked Jacob Eastman's daughter. But Anderson? *Wow*. I almost didn't care about what his reasons were.

"Would you like to see more of me?" He asked.

"Yes."

He looked up then. "I like how you answer questions with no prevarication. I find it very sexy." He picked up the dessert and held out his hand to me. *All in*, I thought as I stood and took it. He led me over to the chaise. He spooned some mousse and held it out to me. I took it slowly.

"That's amazing," I said. "I love chocolate."

"Mmm," he said. He fed me another bite and then kissed me. "Jesus, you taste sweet, Abigail."

"Don't you want any?" I asked.

"I'm not a big lover of sweets. Well, when it comes to food."

I collected some whipped cream on my finger and held it to him anyway. *Two can play this game*. He took my finger into his mouth and sucked slowly, swirling his tongue around my finger.

"You liked that well enough."

He smirked at me and dipped his finger into the mousse. "Your turn, little flower."

I repeated the moves he'd made and was rewarded with a look of pure lust from him.

"This is, without a doubt, the sexiest dessert I've ever had," I said. "So, thank you for it. And for dinner."

He gave me a pleased look. "Ah, little flower, I'm not done with you yet. The night is still young, after all. Time to put my cards on the table."

ANDERSON

I had been alive for over a thousand years, and I had never felt a bolt of lust like the one I did when Abigail sucked chocolate mousse off my finger. I had a sudden image of her on her knees, my cock in her mouth, and my hand in that glorious sable-colored hair.

A handful of times during dinner, I changed my mind about what I was doing. I couldn't bring this woman into my world. She'd been through enough over the last year or so. But then she'd ask a question, laugh, or I'd scent the spice under her sweet and change my mind. She was so smart, and smart women are like catnip to me. I also couldn't recall the last time someone had been genuinely interested in what it was like to be a vampire.

Plus, she wanted me. Of that, I was sure.

But I'd be honest with her. I'd let her know what I wanted and give her a chance to run. And despite myself, I would try and go slowly with her. I had no idea where this attack of conscience came from, but it was inconvenient. I was not a patient man, but I did not want to fuck this up.

I brought our brandies over, and she took a sip. "You said you scented me. What do I smell like?"

"Honeyed lilacs. I cannot explain it better than that. But yesterday," *— had it only been yesterday? —* "I scented something spicier under that. Something new, and once it was there, I couldn't ignore it." I twirled a lock of her hair around my finger. "What were you thinking about?"

"Work," she answered. "That's only partly true. I was also thinking about my father. It hadn't been a good day."

"Ah, I am sorry."

"Why do you bait those old women?" She blurted out.

"Do you know where they go every day?" I wondered when she'd ask that. The timing was odd, but I sensed she was trying to settle her nerves.

"Not for sure, but I'd assume church."

"You are correct. To pray. I'm at an age where I find religion tiresome. Those women pray for me. They've told me that. Our sparring sends them to church every day to pray for the soul of the evil, tatted vampire."

She gave me a steady look. I sighed. "Seeing them each morning assures me they are still alive. I am not sentimental, but I admit I have a soft spot for them." Once again, she'd flustered me by getting me to admit something I barely even told myself.

"Thank you," she said, looking away at the painting on the wall. It was a nude of two people fucking. "Do people use these rooms for that?"

"Yes, sometimes. I charge considerably more if that occurs." I ran a finger down her neck and was delighted at her shiver. I put my lips to her neck. "Are you quite ready to hear what I want from you?"

She nodded. "I am," she said softly, but her voice was steady.

I kissed the back of her neck and pulled her head until it rested against my shoulder. My arm snaked around her waist. I waited. She didn't pull away. I ran my tongue up her neck as my hand made its way to her breast. She whimpered as I rolled her nipple between my fingers, cursing her dress for being in the way.

"Your skin excites me. It's so soft and smooth. I want to tell you what I would like to do to it. May I?"

"Yes." Her voice was even softer than before.

"I want to mark it. I want to bite it. I want to look at your legs, thighs, and belly and know you're mine because I can see my marks on you." My other hand moved to her other nipple, and she arched her back.

"Go on, Anderson. What else do you want to do with me?"

So fucking bold. But not frightened. On the contrary, she was interested, and I could tell by her scent that she was aroused.

"I want my cock in your mouth. I want you to take me so deep that you choke, but you keep taking me in until all of me is in your mouth. Then I want to watch you as my cum shoots down that pretty throat of yours." I pinch her nipples gently, and she cries out. "Do you want me to stop?"

"No. No, I don't. I want you to continue."

I chuckled softly. "Then I am going to fuck you so hard your entire building will hear you screaming my name. I will fuck your mouth, your pussy, and that ass of yours. And I am going to worship every mark on your body. You know one of the best things about vampires?"

"What's that?" She was breathless with need.

"We have amazing stamina. We can fuck again almost immediately. Do you like what I'm telling you, Abigail?"

"I like it. Very much." She paused. "No one has ever spoken to me quite like this."

Good. I was the first, and I was absolutely going to be the last. But I would need to ease into it. I let her breasts go and began to inch her dress up. "It makes me happy I'm the first. You need to be absolutely sure, little flower. Do you want this?" Verbal consent was key.

"I have one question," she said, putting her hand on mine to stop my progress up her leg.

"What's that?"

"This has nothing to do with me being an Eastman, correct? If it is, please don't do this."

I was shocked by her question. It had never occurred to me people would want to get close to her because of her name or father. "Abigail, please do not take this the wrong way, but I honestly don't give a fuck about your last name or your father—or what he did or did not do. I kept away from you for a year, not knowing anything about your father.

And I sure as hell did not know anything about him when I pulled you aside last night."

But this was a bit of a lie. I did give a fuck because what she had gone through enraged me. The fact her company had investigated her made me want to get involved. Something about this whole thing bothered me. A lot. This was a new feeling for me. I didn't want to think about what it meant, but I was ready to pull down every fucking company and every person who did this to her.

"Okay then, I believe you."

"I hope the hard-on grinding into you is also an indication of how I feel."

"It is. I've ruined the mood now, haven't I?"

I laughed. "Not at all," I said. I grazed my teeth across her clavicle, taking care to keep my fangs retracted. She gasped, then melted further into me. She removed her hand from mine and grabbed my leg.

"Fuck this," I said, spinning her around and putting her flat on her back on the chaise. I settled on her and took her mouth in a punishing kiss. I licked, I bit, I sucked. Her hands were on my chest, and she'd thrown one leg over mine. "You taste fucking amazing," I growled at her.

"So do you," she said. She started to unbutton my shirt, and I pulled back. "Do you want my shirt off?" She nodded. I stood and pulled it off me. She gaped at me, licking her lips.

"Oh my," she said.

"You like my tattoos?" I asked.

"I do. How fully tatted are you?"

"Full body, back and front. I have a few spaces that aren't filled in yet. But I am pretty well covered."

She nodded. "I want to see all of them. All of you."

"You will. Soon." I laid back on her, and she started moving her hands all over my torso. I grabbed them and put them above her head, holding them here. "You need to leave your hands here, little flower. I don't have anything to tie them with. Do you understand?"

"I do."

"And you agree?"

"I do, Anderson."

"Okay, we'll see how much of a good girl you can be, baby."

"Yes, Anderson."

Fuck, it was hot when she said my name in that breathy tone of voice. I moved down her body, lifting her dress and spreading her legs. "Lift," I commanded. She did, and I pulled off her lacy blue thong.

"Did you want me to take my shoes off?"

"No, baby, we're going to leave those on." I pushed her dress to her waist and spread her legs farther apart. "Look at you. You're so wet for me, aren't you? God, you're so perfect."

I dropped to my knees and tongued her clit. She screamed and clamped her hand over her mouth. I laughed. "The rooms are soundproofed." And I had made sure the recording devices for this room had been turned off for tonight. "You scream all you want. But don't move those hands."

She nodded and moved her hands back above her head. She threw her head back as I swirled my tongue around her wetness. Sliding two fingers inside her, I pumped roughly, and she moaned my name. "You like it rough like that, or do you want me to be gentle?"

"Rough," She moaned. "God, please, rough."

I kept pumping as I kissed and licked her thighs. "Baby, I want to mark you here. May I?"

"Yes, Anderson. Do it!"

I bit gently, then harder, and she bucked under me. Her wanting this was a wonderful surprise. I kept pumping her, giving her a matching bite on the other side, and she whimpered. I sucked on her clit as I kept a steady rhythm with my fingers, adding a third.

"What do you want, little flower? Do you want to come?" I looked at her. She hadn't moved her hands, but she watched me—her gaze full of desire.

"Yes, Anderson, I want to come. Please make me come."

"Say it again."

"Please, Anderson, please make me come!"

I pumped harder and faster as I licked the bite marks I had just made, sucking on them gently. I put my mouth back on her clit, bit gently, and then pressed my tongue against it. Abigail came apart noisily as I continued to pump her. When her orgasm slowed, I lapped at her with my tongue, building to a second just as noisy orgasm.

When she finally began to breathe normally, our eyes met. And I knew right then, she would be mine. I pulled myself up and kissed her so she could taste herself on my lips.

"You can move your hands now, Abigail."

"Good." She pulled my head back to hers and kissed me hard. I was enthralled with this woman.

I pulled back and stood, reaching a hand out. She took it, and I pulled her up, putting my arms around her. Her hand found its way to my erection, and she ran her hand along it lightly. "Not tonight, Abigail. This was about you. I can wait."

She pulled back. "But I want to."

"And I want you to. Believe me, I do. But there will be time for that." I couldn't say why I hesitated, but I wanted it to be clear this wasn't a one-night event. Denying myself felt like the way to get that point across without voicing it.

"Okay, Anderson. Another time."

I kissed the top of her head. "I am going to do something very out of character,"

"What's that?" she asked, running her hands over my shoulders.

"I am going to take you home now. You like touching, don't you?"

"I haven't touched another man in—I can't tell you how long. Also, you are a feast for the eyes and hands."

Not for the first time tonight, I had to tamp a lid on the feelings she stirred. "I do need to put a shirt on. I can't walk the streets like this."

"Pity," she backed away so that I could dress.

I cleared my throat. "It's been an eventful evening, and I've said a lot. I want to attempt to take things slowly. This is new for you." I thought for a moment. "You'll need to come up with a safe word as well. And I'd like you to research what I've said and what else you want to try."

She nodded. "I do have some ideas." She looked at me. "My thong?"

"I will return it when I get you home."

She rolled her eyes, then yawned. "I am tired," she admitted.

"Then I shall take you home. But we're driving."

"It's five blocks!"

"You want me to give your thong back on the street?"
"Okay, we're driving."

ABIGAIL

I walked into my apartment, took my shoes off, and proceeded to do a happy dance for the next couple of minutes through my living room. It's amazing what a couple of great orgasms can do for your mood. My phone rang, and I answered it without thinking.

"Hello?"

"You know I can see you in the window dancing up there, yes?" An amused voice all but purred in my ear.

I burst out laughing—so much for coming across as sophisticated. "I didn't think about it actually. I didn't think you'd hang around."

"I wanted to make sure you reached your apartment." A car door opened and closed.

"Afraid I might get attacked in the hallway? We do have a doorman."

"Your doorman is practically ancient and fairly useless, aside from opening doors."

He had me there. Marvin had been a doorman here for longer than I'd been alive. And I was forty-one. "Well, as you can see, I am safe in my apartment and would like to get back to my impromptu dance party."

"Of course, Abigail. I have a question, though. You may not like it."

"Ask anyway. I don't have to answer it."

"Your CFO is the one who ordered your work to be investigated. I have to wonder why, based on how you handled your father's things once he went into prison."

How to answer this? Mason Deveraux didn't like me. He wanted to fuck me, and that fact pissed him off. To him, I should be beneath his notice. Mason was single, never married, and from what I could tell, didn't date much. I suspected he paid for it, and I support sex work, so I had no problem with that. I hope they charged him a lot. But over the last year, he treated me, a senior accounting VP with a law degree, like I should be willing to take whatever he handed me, even if it was his cock. I was ten times smarter than he was, and he knew I would be better at his job. This was his way of putting me in my place. Who would hire the daughter of a convicted felon? But do I tell Anderson that? Especially when we'd just begun ... whatever this was.

"Abigail, your lack of response tells me that the answer is something I will not like. Am I correct?"

"Yes, you are. The little I know you, I can tell you won't like this."

"Tell me anyway, little flower." So, I did. He was silent for a good long while. "You are correct. I don't like it. Not one bit. Why do you put up with it?"

I didn't want to put all my cards on the table yet. So, I told him part of the truth and hoped he wouldn't hear what I didn't say. "Because my father was convicted of embezzlement. Who would be willing to hire his daughter? I managed to hang onto this job, and until I can figure out another way, here I sit." I paused. "Plus, it pisses him off how good I am at it."

He laughed softly. "Thank you for telling me."

"Are you going to kill him?" I asked.

"Not tonight, little flower. Get some rest." He ended the call.

Well, that didn't put me at ease.

I changed into something comfortable and went into my office. Dressing up was nice, but at heart, I was a jeans and t-shirt kind of gal. I popped a soda open while waiting for the laptop to boot up. I wasn't tired, so I might as well do some work.

This had nothing to do with my job, so the best time to do it was late at night. My father wasn't guilty. I knew he wasn't. But his CFO,

Marc Jennings, was. And somehow, my CFO was involved as well. I have been doing this with most of my evenings for the last few months.

When Dad first went to prison, I was too busy handling things to think this through. He had asked me to sell the apartment and anything valuable to make restitution. He'd also implored me to find the files. At least, that's what I thought he'd said to me. It had been chaos in the courtroom. I had forgotten about it until one night when I couldn't sleep. I had known dad was doing a quiet investigation into Jennings. He shared that with me, and I saw the files on his computer, along with his handwritten notes.

I knew I needed to get into his company's computer systems. It took me a while to remember, but when I interned there in college, none of the interns or temp workers had personal logins. They were all generic. The passwords also had a formula for them. It was a security nightmare, but the CEO refused to authorize changing it. Nothing had changed, and I was able to get in.

Finding anything, though, was difficult. The logins could only find so much. I had only gotten this far because I had worked in the IT department while interning, and they had shared some tricks with me. Still, I tried again and found a couple of recently opened files. They'd been copied to a network drive anyone could see. Someone was going to get in trouble for that. I downloaded them quickly before they disappeared. *Shit*! They were encrypted.

I needed a computer hacker. But I had no idea how you even found one.

My father had done something with all his info, but what?

I opened my email and saw Lacey was online. I pinged her, and she called me immediately.

"Why aren't you getting fucked into next week right now?"

I laughed. "He's taking it slow. So, he says. What are you still doing up?"

"Peter is away for the night, and I can't sleep without him. It's gross." But there was affection in her voice. She and her husband adored each other. If she wasn't sleeping, neither was he.

"Phone sex?" I asked.

"We did that earlier," she replied. "Now, spill."

I told her about the evening, leaving details out, but she got the general gist.

"I am so happy right now. I am bouncing up and down!" I could picture her doing that. "You needed some good in your life."

"Is this good, though? I mean, it feels very intense, very quickly."

"What did I tell you the first time I saw Peter?"

"Well, when you could speak again, you said you'd be marrying him within the year."

"And did I?"

"You did!" I affirmed.

"And had I ever said anything like that before?"

"Only in second grade when you insisted you were going to marry Brad Winston. You said he brought the good chips in for lunch."

"I can't believe you remember that! But my point stands."

"What is your point exactly?"

"Sometimes it's just right from the get-go. You just know."

"It's too soon to know anything."

"Whatever. Stop doing your corporate espionage shit and go to bed."

"Only if you do."

"Fine, I'll go to bed. Love you, Abs."

"Love you, Lacey." I took her advice and went to bed.

ANDERSON

I decided to do some research on Jacob Eastman myself. He hadn't been born wealthy; he'd and grew up downtown. His family had owned an electronics store. Again, that tingling was at the back of my head, but I couldn't place why.

He'd been a wunderkind with numbers, rising through corporate America easily and quickly. But quietly. He wasn't showy but careful about his chosen companies. He mostly stayed with smaller companies, helping them, then moving on until Allied Tech offered him a senior VP position.

Abigail's mother died when her daughter was only sixteen, and all I could think was Jacob wanted something more stable so he could finish raising his daughter and send her to a decent college. He had wanted her to have opportunities he hadn't had growing up.

There was nothing to indicate Jacob was a thief. Companies did well under him, and everyone he worked with liked and respected him. Except for the CFO at Allied, it seems. I have always been able to sniff out when someone was dipping their hand where it didn't belong. It's a skill I honed over centuries working with my *abeoji*. Father had drilled into all of us what to look for. Jacob Eastman was not a thief.

Jacob's trial was quick. Too quick. I found that strange. But the further I dug into it, the one thing that didn't make sense to me was

Abigail had not needed to sell anything of hers to make restitution. Her father's wealth was a thing of public record, and the sale of his assets more than covered the funds required.

So why had she done it? She was fine with people thinking she'd helped her father make good, but I didn't buy it. I had trouble believing she would so easily resign herself to an internal investigation. It was possible, I barely knew her after all, but I didn't buy it.

I have loved puzzles since I was a child in Korea, and my long life has made me quite good at them. I'd figure this one out as well. Something was going on under the surface. I hoped my little flower wasn't in over her head.

I emailed Jack overnight with the information Abigail had shared about Mason Deveraux and Marc Jennings. I wanted to have a little talk with Deveraux and asked Jack to find him for me.

Early Sunday, he called. "Boss, Mason Deveraux is playing squash this morning at his club."

"People still play squash?" I did not understand humans sometimes.

Jack's voice was amused when he answered. "They do."

"Well, we need to speak with Deveraux."

"I thought you might feel that way. Who do you want to bring?"

"Soames and Keith did well with their tasks last night. Let's bring them along today. See how they do with looking menacing."

"The sunglasses will help. I will be there in twenty. Soames and Keith will meet us there."

"Jack, have you contacted them already?"

"I thought you may choose them, so I gave them a heads up."

"Well done. I don't pay you enough."

"Anderson, you pay me an obscene amount of money."

"Well, we may need to make that a *really* obscene amount of money. I will see you in twenty minutes."

***

When we stepped into Deveraux's upscale gym, all activity ground to a halt. It was hardly ever a good sign if I showed up someplace unexpectedly. Even if people don't know who I am, they know a predator when they see one. Everyone there was hoping I wasn't there for them.

Jack walked to the front desk. "Mason Deveraux."

"Sir?" The young man at the counter asked, his eyes darting to me, then the two vampires standing behind me.

"I thought I was clear. Mason Deveraux. Where is he?"

"Sir, I am sorry, but I don't think I can tell you that."

Jack sighed. "Fine, we can do this the hard way." He stepped away from the desk, and I walked to it.

"You will tell me where Mason Deveraux is right now, or you will live to regret it." He stared at me. "Son, you do not get paid enough to tell me no. I have to assume, based on the look on your face, that you recognize me?" He nodded. "Wonderful. Then tell me where he is. He is the only one I am here for. And as long as everyone else stays out of the way, no one else will get hurt."

He checked the computer quickly. "His squash game just got done. He's likely in the locker room or showers." He handed me a key. "Master key." Now that was a touch I appreciated. I gestured at Jack, who stepped back to the desk and peeled off ten one-hundred-dollar bills, sliding them to the young man—a little money now, a little loyalty later, if needed.

"I appreciate your help and the key. You saw nothing."

"I don't know what you mean, sir. Is someone here?"

"Good lad," I said. I assumed that his initial refusal was so that he could tell his boss he had tried, so he could cover his ass. I had seen this many times before, and respected it. But I always get my way, and this time was no exception. He pointed us in the right direction, and we made our way to the locker room. Everyone gave us a wide berth.

"That's him over there," said Jack. I looked over at a man in his mid-sixties with a hefty paunch. He was balding and had decided that a combover was the way to handle it. Beady eyes and a patchy beard rounded out his appearance. He smelled putrid.

I frankly found it offensive that this person thought he was good enough to be in Abigail's presence, let alone thinking he had any right to want to touch her.

"Gentlemen," Jack announced to the room. "I am afraid I need everyone, except Mr. Deveraux, to leave. Immediately." The room stilled, and everyone looked at us, then Mason. For his part, Mason looked close to vomiting.

"Now, gentlemen!" Jack barked. I sometimes gave Jack a hard time, but I sincerely hoped he would turn vampire. He is one of the best seconds I have ever had. A former Marine, tough as nails and smart as hell. The room emptied quickly.

Jack motioned to Soames and Keith, who went over to Mason and pushed him into a chair. This gym was so fancy; it had leather armchairs in it. Ridiculous.

"Look, I don't know what this is about it, but I haven't done any-thing!" Mason squeaked. I rolled my eyes before I took my sunglasses off.

"You know who I am, yes?" I asked.

He nodded. "I do, yes. And may I say ..."

"No, you may not say anything." His mouth shut quickly. "I would like to talk to you about Abigail Eastman."

"What about her? What has she done? I knew she was trouble."

I walked to him and slapped him hard. "I'm sorry, did you say something?"

And because Mason was obviously an idiot, he doubled down. "Abigail Eastman? She's a thief like her father. I can't prove it, but I know it!"

"Lift him," I told my two vampires. They each grabbed an arm and lifted him. I slapped him. "Mason, you are pissing me off. A smart man would have known to keep his mouth shut."

"I don't understand!" He wailed.

"Yes, you do. You instigated an internal investigation against a Senior VP of accounting. Her team is the best you've ever had. I've seen the numbers, Mason." Jack had also been doing his research and relayed this information to me in the car on the drive over. "Now, I want to know why."

"Why? Why? Are you some kind of fucking idiot?" I sighed and slapped him. "Why do you keep slapping me?"

"Because if you're going to act like a little bitch, I will treat you like one." Men like Deveraux find an open-handed slap humiliating. "Trust me, you will experience such pain when I finally decide to kill you. But for now, I want an answer to my question."

He went to put his hand to his cheek, but my two helpers grabbed his arms and held them. That pleased me. The training was often difficult, but these two had good instincts.

"Her father had just been convicted of fraud and embezzlement. They're related. What was I supposed to think?"

"That an employee who ran regular internal audits on the accounting and finance divisions with a clean record was an asset to your company. Additionally, you have been stirring up trouble and shit-talking Jacob Eastman for years. Yet, you hired his daughter."

"That was the former CFO. I would never have. She thinks too much of herself."

Which means she didn't want to fuck him and told him so. I punched him in the stomach, and he bent over, gasping for air. "Who paid you?" I asked, following a hunch.

He lifted his face, his eyes sliding away before sliding back to me. And that was all the admission of guilt I needed. I couldn't kill him yet. I needed him to lead me to the person paying him—the person who started all of this.

"No ... no one. I don't know what you're talking about!"

"Yes, you do. Who is paying you? Who are you working with?"

"No one. Jacob Eastman is garbage. His daughter is ..." I moved so fast he had no time to react. I lifted him off the floor and pinned him against the wall, my hand around his neck.

"It would be so easy to kill you. All I need to do is squeeze. Just a little, and I could shut off your air." I tightened my hold fractionally, and his eyes widened in fear. "Just like that, Mason. If I squeeze a little more, you'd have so little time to live. I'd sit here and watch the life leave your eyes, and it wouldn't bother me. And honestly, Mason, no one else would truly care."

He scrabbled at my hand, trying to speak. "What is it, Mason? Have something to tell me?" I loosened my grip.

"Jennings," he gasped. "Marc Jennings."

"The CFO of Power Dynamics. What about him?"

"He had it out for Eastman. Look there."

And Jennings would blame Deveraux, I am sure. I nodded and let Mason go. He dropped to the floor. I'd let him think I believed him. What he didn't know was, at this moment, his home, car, and office were being bugged. We also set up trackers on his computers to gain access to his email.

"See? That wasn't so hard, was it?" I helped him up. "Mason, the Eastmans are now under my protection. If I hear you say anything about them, I will know. And I will kill you."

"Okay, absolutely. Whatever you say." He was trying to save himself, but it was too late.

"And to make sure you take the lesson to heart," I looked at Soames and Keith. "Rough him up. He should still be able to walk out on his own, but I want visible bruises."

"Absolutely, boss!" Keith replied.

I turned to leave when Mason said, "Can't even do your own dirty work, huh? Fucking pussy."

I turned around. "You won't bait me this way. My people are an extension of my power. But believe this, when I kill you, and I will, I will do it myself." I looked at Soames. "He loses teeth for that. Front ones."

She nodded, and I walked out, Jack behind me.

Back in the car, Jack turned to me. "Jennings?"

"I want all the same surveillance on him. I am not going to visit him yet. Deveraux will call him immediately because Mason is not the brains here. Plus, I want Jennings on edge about a visit from me." The fear of something is often worse for people than when it happens.

He nodded. "Are you going to discuss this with Miss Eastman?"

"I am. I don't want her to have any surprises from him. She knows more about this than she is letting on. I want to know what she knows."

"Should we drop you there now?"

"Please."

On the drive over, Jack received audio of Mason calling Jennings. "Jennings, it's not funny! Fuck!" An odd slurping indicated Mason was slobbering on himself due to those missing teeth. "That fucking vampire is a psychopath. He had my front teeth knocked out."

"I am surprised," Jack put in. "That he made the call with missing teeth."

"I'm not. He's frightened, and he's not thinking things through. And he wants to whine. He wants Jennings to fix it, but I am betting he won't do anything. Deveraux is expendable."

"Mason," said Jennings. "What did you tell him?" Thank goodness Mason was using his speaker function so that we could hear Jennings as well.

"Not a damned thing! But that Eastman bitch knows something. Why else would the vampire sniffing around?" He was trying to cover his ass. "She's been poking around, asking questions, wanting to speak to the board!" I raised an eyebrow. What *was* Abigail up to?

"Don't worry about her. Should we need to take care of her, it will be very easy," Jennings said with a cold-blooded matter-of-factness I did not like.

"The vampire ..."

"Will be absolutely no problem. He'll tire of her. We need to be patient. Anderson Jeon is known to be mercurial when it comes to humans."

"Am I?" I asked Jack.

Jack shrugged. "Not really. People who don't know you may think that. The rest of us do not. As for women, you don't tend to gravitate to human ones, so that's a non-starter. At least not before now."

"You don't think she's on to us?" Mason was having trouble speaking with missing teeth.

"No, and I don't see how Jeon could be either. He was gone too long and is too busy playing restauranter. He's grasping at straws and trying to make a play for our companies. She moved into that shitty apartment downtown because her father was guilty, and she was ashamed. Nothing else."

"He's too arrogant to believe otherwise," I said. "It would never occur to him that anyone who wasn't male or white could best him. He will learn differently." I had earned the right to be arrogant over the centuries. A vampire was the apex predator in most scenarios. And as such, I could be patient.

"Jennings, I am not about to put my ass on the line for this," Mason made a sound like spitting.

"Mason, go find a dentist and leave the thinking to me. I'll kill Abigail Eastman myself if I must." The audio ended.

I sat stone still, staring straight ahead as I mastered my temper. I could flip this car with Jack and our driver, Randy, in it if I wanted to. But I wouldn't. I would not let my anger get the better of me. I was too well-trained for that.

"Anderson?"

"I am trying to calm down," I said through gritted teeth.

Jack nodded. "Good. We've arrived at her apartment." Jack looked out the window. "This is a perfectly decent street and a good building. She even has a doorman. Leave it to someone like Jennings to think this is shitty. *Asshole*. Now the neighborhood I grew up in? That was shitty."

I looked at Jack as he didn't often talk about his childhood. Like mine, I assumed the less said, the better.

"Are you positive you are going to discuss this with her?" He asked me. "You could take care of it, and she'd never know.

"I realize that. But she put herself in their crosshairs for a reason. She's working some angle here, I'm sure of it, and I don't think taking that away from her would be fair." I wanted to discuss this puzzle with her, but more than that, I wanted to see and touch her. Additionally, a big part of me was furious she was putting herself in harm's way. It was not rational, and I did not appreciate the feeling. The sooner this got dealt with, the better.

Jack raised an eyebrow at me. "Well, this is new."

"Isn't it?" I replied.

ABIGAIL

I slept late and had coffee in bed while doing some research on phone about what I might be interested in trying with Anderson. I have always enjoyed sex and liked to think I was adventurous. In the past, I had been game to try things. Some men I'd been with liked that, some didn't. The ones that didn't were encouraged to move on quickly. But with Anderson, I'd be able to indulge myself in a way I hadn't before. The idea was intoxicating. So why not see what I might be interested in trying? Clearly, I didn't mind being marked, which was a surprise. I enjoyed seeing his marks on my inner thighs—quite a bit.

After a while, I got turned on. I stopped scrolling and looked toward the bottom drawer of my night table. I hadn't been with anyone in a long time by choice, so I had stocked a wide array of toys to take care of myself. Anderson had not told me not to touch myself, so I felt at liberty. I opened the drawer and pulled something out at random. I got comfortable and thought about Anderson. Watching him with his head between my legs last night was so hot. And the way he'd talked to me ... What he said. I'd almost come just from that.

I spread my legs further and moved the toy faster, chasing my orgasm.

BAM! BAM! BAM!

I jerked. *What the fuck?* Who was banging on my door on a Sunday morning? I was going to ignore it, but the banging continued. I stomped to the living room and realized I had a skimpy nightgown on. I grabbed a coat, held it in front of me, grabbed my home defense baseball bat, and pulled the door open, ready to give someone hell.

Anderson stood on the other side. He looked pissed off, and in my surprise, the coat fell away from me. I dropped the bat. He took me in, and I knew what he saw; a barely-there nightgown, bedhead, eyes that still had desire in them, and he could scent my arousal. He stormed into the apartment, nostrils flared as his head swiveled around the space, as if he was looking for something. Or someone maybe.

Shit! Did he think someone was here? I quickly shut and locked the door, moving in front of him. "Anderson," I said, putting my hands on his chest.. He was reacting, not thinking. "Stop!" I didn't know what to do, so I stood on his feet and cupped his face with my hands. "Anderson, think. No one is here. You'd be able to scent them. It's just me."

He took a shuddering breath, then another, until his temper settled. "I apologize. I jumped to conclusions."

"You did." I stepped off his feet. "I am going to let it go and forgive you this time. Please don't do it again." If it happened again, it would be a problem.

He nodded and backed up, looking at me. His eyes gleamed. "What have you been up to this morning, little flower?" I looked at him and blushed. "I think I know." He started down the hallway, obviously looking for my bedroom.

Shit! "Anderson!" I raced after him. When I got to my bedroom, he was leaning over my bed with my toy in his hand. He stood and looked at me, a speculative gleam in his eye. I should have asked him why he barged in here, but I could ask later. Right now, the way he was looking at me, *damn!*

"My, my," he said. "Aren't we a filthy little angel? Were you pleasuring yourself?" I nodded. "Words, Abigail, use them. I will ask you again. Were you pleasuring yourself when I knocked?"

"Yes, Anderson." I had a boyfriend who tried this kind of talk with me once, and I laughed. I was not laughing now. I was trying to keep from melting into a puddle.

"What were you thinking about?"

"You," I answered. There was no point in lying. Whatever was about to happen, I wanted.

He walked over to me, the toy still in his hand. He reached under my nightie and stroked the marks on my thighs. "Were you thinking about these?"

"Yes, Anderson."

He smiled predatorily. And I couldn't breathe suddenly. He handed me the toy. "Show me, baby."

"Wh ... what?"

"Show me how you get yourself off." He took off his jacket and rolled up his sleeves. "I am going to watch you."

I had never done that before, masturbated in front of someone else. This was hot. I went to lie down, and I heard his voice. "Nightie off, baby. I want to see your body while you do it." I did as he asked and climbed onto the bed.

He pulled the armchair around to watch me from the best angle. He sat with his long legs spread out in front of him. "You do what you would normally do."

I nodded. I didn't need to work myself up; I was already there. I flicked the toy on and used it on my clit, spreading my legs further apart so he had a good view. "Fuck," He muttered, his eyes intent on me. I took one nipple and pinched it. He groaned.

"Jesus, Abigail. Look at you. Look how fucking beautifully dirty you are. I can see how wet you are from here." He stroked himself lightly over his pants. "You see how hard I am for you, don't you, baby?" I didn't say anything. "Don't you, little flower?" He snapped out.

"Yes, Anderson," I moaned as I moved the toy faster.

"I am going to enjoy thinking about you doing this to yourself, how you make yourself come thinking about me, about what I have done to you, and what I am going to fucking do to you."

"What," I breathe, "What do you plan to do to me?"

"Everything, little flower. But right now, I need you to bear down on that clit of yours and make yourself come. I want to watch you come apart. The next time, that will be my cock inside you."

I moved quicker, pinching my nipple harder until I arched off the bed and came on a moan. My eyes close as a hand takes away the toy. His fingers, bringing a second one on. When it's over, I open my eyes and find him watching me. He has an odd expression on his face. Desire, but something else is mingled there, and I realize it's wonder.

He shakes himself out of it, standing and licking me off his fingers. He toes out of his shoes and socks, then unbuttons his pants and takes those off, and then his shirt. He is absolutely fucking perfect.

I get off the bed and move to him. He only has a handful of clear spaces, and even with those, he takes my breath away. He's that beautiful. I move my hands over his chest, back, and perfect ass. "I take it you're pleased?"

I look him in the eye. "You are, hands down, the most beautiful being I have ever seen in my life."

He smiles at me—a genuinely pleased smile. "The tattoos meet your expectations, then?"

I nod. "Oh, yes!" I stroked his torso, running my tongue along his chest and back. He pulls me in front of him, winding my hair in his hand, and crushes his mouth to mine. The kiss is savage as he licks, bites, and sucks. I grip his shoulders and grind myself against him like a cat in heat.

He tears his mouth away from mine. "Since I cannot get you pregnant or give you anything, I would like to fuck that pussy bare."

"Yes, yes, please!" I've never done that with anyone. This was a nice perk of being with a vampire, no worries about pregnancy or diseases. The fact we'd be doing this bare excited me.

"Safe word, little flower?"

"Oh, yes. 'Mustang.'" He gives me a quizzical look. "It was the first car I owned." He nods his head. The only one I had ever owned. Selling it had been difficult.

He pulls my antique standing mirror near the bed and stands behind me, cupping my breasts.

"Look at us," he commands. I do. "Have you ever watched yourself get fucked?" I shake my head. "Good, I was hoping to be the first." He moves in front of me, taking a nipple in his mouth and playing with the other. "So fucking beautiful. So fucking dirty. Like you were made for me."

He crouches, kissing my stomach, then moves my legs apart to lick my clit. I close my eyes, but he pinches my ass.

"Look at us in the mirror, Abigail." I did. It was so hot to watch him. He stood, and I immediately dropped to my knees. "What are you doing down there?" he asked, amused.

"Your turn to watch," I said as I licked the precum off the tip of his cock and then took it in my mouth. He hissed but watched us in the mirror.

I took more of him until he groaned, "That's enough. I am not coming down your throat this time."

He sat on the bed and pulled me to him so I faced the mirror. He shifted and then shifted me so his cock was lined with my sex. "Are you ready for me to fuck you?"

"Yes, Anderson."

"It's so fucking hot when you say it that way." He growled and thrust his hips until he was inside me. I screamed and dug my nails into his thighs. "That's right, my filthy angel, you can mark me too."

We both moved, our eyes pinned to the reflection of us fucking in the mirror. I never knew what people meant when they said sex with someone ruined them for others. I got it now. I don't think anyone would ever make me feel like this again.

One hand cupped my breast as he licked and sucked my skin. He bit gently on the back of my neck, and I arched. "It's such a turn-on that you like when I do that, little flower. I like that as much as seeing the marks on your skin."

I moaned and rocked on him as he thrust into me harder, rougher. His hand on my breast tightened, and his other found its way to my clit. It felt so good. I closed my eyes, and he stopped. My eyes snapped open.

"You keep those eyes on us in the mirror. I don't want to stop again. I want you to see yourself come."

He took my clit between his fingers and rubbed as I grabbed my other breast. "Anderson, *God*, that feels so good."

"I know it does. Pinch your nipple. The way you like to do it." His fingers moved swiftly on my clit as his cock pounded me faster. His other hand went to my neck. He stopped briefly to look at me, a question in his eyes, and I nodded at him.

"Yes," I said. "Do it." His hand circled my neck gently, and I moved faster on him. There was nothing but the echo of slapping bodies as I came closer to orgasm. "Anderson!"

"That's the way, Abigail. Be a good girl, and come on my cock now. So fucking wet for me, you're practically dripping. And it's going to feel so good to come."

He thrust and bore down on my clit, and I screamed his name as I came. He kept working my clit and moving inside me as my orgasm ran through me, and he chased his. His hands drifted to my waist, moving me on his cock faster until I was able to match the rhythm.

Finally, he roared and came inside me. It felt fucking amazing. I sagged against him, and his arms wrapped around my waist as his nose pressed into my neck. If I had known what this would be like, I wouldn't have spent a year trying to make myself invisible. Damn!

***

Later, after we'd cleaned up, we were back in bed. I was on my stomach, resting my head on my arms as Anderson lazily stroked my back. It wasn't sexual, but something else I couldn't—or didn't—want to name.

I looked at him. "Not used to this, are you?"

He looked at me. "Abigail, I assure you I've had sex before."

I laughed. "I don't mean that. I mean, sticking around. I don't think you stay and cuddle as a rule."

"No, that is true," he replied. "But I am quite content at the moment."

I smiled. I noticed one spot devoid of tattoos was over his heart and traced the outline. I felt a little sad. Not having something meaningful enough to place over your heart was a bit of a tragedy after so many centuries. Then again, I didn't really know Anderson, apart from his

44

ability to give great orgasms. What he chose to put, or not put, over his heart was none of my business.

"So, why were you pounding on my door on a Sunday morning?" I was sure he got past the doorman the same way the vampire who brought the wine had.

"Well, I ran into someone you know today. Mason Deveraux."

"Oh?" I was suddenly on full alert. Mason being my boss and all.

"Yes. And I believe I know what you're up to, Abigail. You're investigating Mason and the CFO of your father's company. I am sure of it. Which means you believe your father to be innocent of any wrongdoing. But I am really curious why you think it's fine to put yourself in danger by taking this on by yourself?"

I sat and looked at him. There was fury in his gaze, though I wasn't sure why. Why did it matter to him what I did? I stood and grabbed my fluffy robe. "I am not going to deny it. There's no point. But if we're going to discuss it, I need food as I've not eaten today."

He got up and grabbed his pants. "It's afternoon. How have you not eaten yet?"

"Well, someone interrupted me this morning. Not that I minded, of course." I loved food, but set mealtimes were not my thing. I ate when I was hungry, and I rarely ate when I first got up in the morning.

"No breakfast?"

"Look, Dad, I eat when I'm hungry!" His eyes widened at my words, and his lips twitched. Dad is very close to Daddy. There are times when I have more mouth than sense. Today is one of those times. "Anyway, I am now hungry. So, food!"

I marched off to the kitchen with him chuckling as he followed behind me. He sat on the other side of the island. "You know, if you want to call me Daddy ..."

"Stop right there! Just stop!" I pulled out the eggs, mushrooms, spinach, cheese, and leeks. I also pulled out the bacon. "Do you want to split an omelet with me?"

"That would be lovely," he said.

"Bacon?"

"Bacon is also good. May I help?"

I turned to look at him. "You cook?"

"No, but I am able to assist."

"Uh-huh. No, that's fine. Something to drink? Coffee? Tea? Water?"

"I do not drink coffee. Wine would be nice."

I gaped at him. "No coffee? Is that a vampire thing?"

"No, it's a me thing. I do like tea, though."

"Good to know. Okay, wine it is, then." I poured some wine. "Now, what do you want to know?" I paused. "And why do you think I am in danger?"

ANDERSON

To say that Abigail surprised me at every turn would be an understatement. From the moment she opened the door in that skimpy piece of cloth, to right now, with her cooking for us, she upended my expectations.

And Christ, that piece of silk she'd been wearing ... A warm pink that brought out the blush on her skin. I could smell her arousal immediately. And I jumped to the wrong conclusion. I reacted in a way I had not for centuries, and it weighed on me. Watching her as she made herself come almost undid me, as had watching us in the mirror. But the biggest surprise by far was how relaxed I was in her bed afterward. I had not lied to her; I was quite content to be there with her.

And now she was cooking for us. I enjoyed watching her prepare the vegetables, whisk the eggs, and cook the bacon. Even in that ridiculous robe she had put on, she was extraordinary.

"Anderson?" She asked. "Are you there?"

I snapped myself out of my thoughts. "I am, yes." I took a sip of wine to collect myself. "Am I correct? Are you trying to investigate your boss?"

Abbie paused her chopping and sighed. "Yes," she said, resuming her work. "I am."

"Is it because you believe your father to be innocent?"

Her head snapped up, and she glared at me. "I know he's innocent!"

I held up my hand. "Peace, Abigail. I am not here to argue that point. You believe Deveraux and Jennings to be involved?" She nodded, putting the vegetables in a pan. "Is that the real reason you moved downtown?"

"Yes, though, I am happy here." She turned the bacon and continued. "It was handy for people to think I was ashamed, and that's why I moved here. Like being here was a scarlet A on my chest. Such bullshit. We lived downtown for years before Jennings hired my dad, and we were happy here!"

"Did you?" he asked. "You weren't born with a silver spoon in your mouth?"

"No, I wasn't. I assumed you knew that. Dad's family owned a small business, but it struggled a fair bit. My mom was born into a wealthy family, but she met my dad in college. Her parents hated him, so they cut her out of their lives. He was both working-class, in their opinion, and Jewish, two unforgivable things."

"I'm sorry." I was surprised to find I meant it.

"Thank you. I tried to contact them when she was dying, but they hung up on me—twice."

"Are they still alive?" I asked casually.

Abigail smiled at me. "They aren't. You can't kill or ruin them, I'm afraid. I do have an uncle. You can ruin him if you'd like. He also hung up on me. Three times."

"Alright," I answered mildly.

"I was kidding."

"I wasn't."

She looked at me. "Don't kill him, please."

"Why not?"

"Because if you ruined him, he would have to live a long time with the shame of being ruined and forgotten by everyone he knows."

"I cannot tell if you're joking or not."

"The problem is, neither can I. My mother loved her parents and worshipped her brother. Their abandonment was a wound that never quite healed. My father doesn't have a bitter bone in his body. Even now. Me? I am bitter and angry." She removed the bacon from the pan and poured the grease into a tin coffee can. She then popped two English muffins into the toaster oven and poured the eggs into the pan with the vegetables. "Anyway, I moved downtown and submitted to that sham of an investigation, hoping they'd think I would behave."

"While you covertly began investigating your boss and Jennings?"

"Yup. My father suspected something was going on, and he had been looking into this for ages. He had run all the numbers. But I can't find those files, and I honestly don't know how far he got."

"Did you see this information?"

"I did." She flipped the omelet, folded it over, and then slid it onto the cutting board to cut it in half. She then went about fixing our plates. She brought them over to a small bistro table by the window. I picked up our glasses and the wine bottle and moved to sit. She got butter and jam and sat across from me.

It was all horrifyingly domestic. And I loved every fucking minute of it. I took a bite of the omelet. "This is very good. Thank you for cooking."

"You're welcome. Now tell me, how much shit did you get me into with Deveraux? And you still need to tell me why you think I'm in danger."

"They suspect you know something."

"Fuck, Anderson!"

I shrugged. "I would tell you I was sorry, but I'm not. There is a good chance they suspected you before I stepped in." I was sure of it. "You are out of your league, Abigail. Jennings was talking about killing you."

Her fork clattered on her plate. "How do you know that?"

I told her the entire story, including how I had his front teeth knocked out.

She took a bite of bacon. "You're right then. He must have suspected me before you involved yourself." Her tone was mild but slightly chiding. "I didn't ask to speak to the board, though. I asked a member if I could speak with them privately. And it looks like she went and told Deveraux. So much for women sticking together. Bitch."

"Who is this board member?" Abigail shook her head. "I can find out with or without you."

"Fine! Miranda Summers. She talked a good game about us needing to stick together as women and how she hated that they investigated me. But in reality, she likes to speak down to me. I allowed it, thinking she might still help. I'd like to tear her fucking head off right now."

"We can manage that."

"I need to watch what I say around you," she said, sipping wine. "I'm blowing off steam."

"Hmmm, perhaps. So, these files that have disappeared, do you know when?"

"I saw them before Dad was arrested. He didn't share them with me. I happened to see them one night on his computer. I forgot about them with the chaos of the trial. When he was being taken away, we hugged, and he told me to find the answers. I assumed he meant the files. I searched his personal laptop, which they never got because it was with me. I even searched mine. Then I tried to find a thumb drive, but nothing."

"Safety deposit box? Something like that?"

"Dad didn't have one. Everything he had got sold to make restitution and pay fees. Well, everything I didn't sneak out during the trial. His apartment, paintings, some first edition books, things like that. I knew people were watching, so I made a show of it. I did as thorough a search as I could while doing it."

"The story is you sold your apartment and belongings to cover what was owed."

"I circulated that story. His stuff more than took care of that. I sold my artwork so he'd have money to help restart his life when he was released. I sold the apartment because you do that when you move somewhere else. People are idiots."

"You let them think you were going to slum it because they're snobs about downtown. You knew that about them and used the information to your advantage."

"Exactly. I always suspected those two. They hated my father. Jennings's predecessor was the one that hired him—same thing happened with me. My father should have gotten the CFO position. Everyone was surprised when Jennings did."

"Your father wasn't angry?" I found this surprising.

"He's never angry. Not even now. He's sitting in prison because he was framed, but he's not angry. He didn't get angry when Mom died. Oh, he mourned her, and he was heartbroken. But it never made him angry that she was gone."

"It made you angry, though," Not a question. Abigail was bristling with fury. I could feel it, and I could smell it. That's the spice under that sweet scent of hers—her anger. One puzzle solved.

"Fuck yes, it made me angry. I was sixteen, and cancer took my mom from me! And these assholes took my dad, for greed, for spite, and I fucking hate it!" Her voice broke.

I hooked my leg around her chair and pulled it closer to me. I then plucked her out of it and put her on my lap, wrapping my arms around her. I am not one to give comfort, but I did not like seeing her upset. I was trying not to dwell on how much I didn't like it, as this was not the time to examine my own feelings. One thing was clear, Abigail was angry at the world, and the world would pay. I'd make sure of that.

"Fuck!" she said, trying not to cry. "I am so goddamned furious!"

"I know, little flower. But I don't think you should do this alone."

She took a deep breath. "You just met me, and you're offering to help me?"

"You and I have been watching each other for a year now."

"In passing." But she leaned against me, stroking my arm as if the act gave her comfort.

"It doesn't matter. That spicy scent under the sweetness was your anger, and it broke through my reticence about you. I can't ignore it. And while you are brilliant, this is dangerous. You could use a vampire's assistance."

"I could go find another vampire," she said.

I tightened my hold and growled. "I don't fucking think so!"

"I'm teasing, Anderson. What made you so reticent originally?"

"Your scent was so sweet, it made me wary like you were untouchable. Especially with the way you tried to make yourself invisible. Why did you?"

"You scared the fuck out of me."

"You thought I'd hurt you?"

"Quite the opposite. I wanted you, and I knew I wouldn't be able to say no. I wouldn't even want to say no."

I gave her a smug smile. "Of course, you wouldn't."

She smacked my arm. "Don't gloat. You know you're a sex god." She laughed. And that was better than tears any day.

"So, are you going to let me help?" I asked her.

"Yes, because I *am* in over my head. I don't want Jennings to hurt me. I want to free my dad. And they should pay."

"I agree, they should." Jennings, Deveraux, Summers, and her fucking uncle while I was at it. "You should call in sick tomorrow, then work from home the rest of the week. Is that possible?"

"It is, yes. It will make Deveraux suspicious, though."

"He already is. I want him running scared. If I can get you access to his, Jennings's, and Summers's finances, will you review them for anomalies?"

"I will. I wish we knew where Dad's files were. Unless they were destroyed."

"I don't think they were. Jennings may have them, and he strikes me as the type to keep trophies of his kills. Arrogant fuck."

"Makes sense," she said. She started to rise, but I held her in place. "I'm okay now."

"I know. I like having you on my lap." I moved her hair aside and kissed the back of her neck. She shivered, and I smiled. "Would you object to me bringing Jack in? He's my second in command."

"Sure," she said. "That's fine. I assume he's been the one finding the information for you?"

"Some of it. But I also have been doing my own research. I'll phone him in a little bit."

"Are you watching Jennings and Deveraux or something?"

"Deveraux, as of now, yes. Jennings will be next. We should probably do the same with this Summers woman."

"Okay," she replied simply. "I have a completely unrelated question."

"Ask away," I took a sip of wine, then offered her my glass. She took a sip from it. This pleased me.

"Why do you stand outside your restaurant in the mornings and evenings like you do? You explained the old women, but you are always out there."

"My apartment is above the restaurant," I said.

"It is? Just yours?"

"Just mine. I own the building."

"Handy. But that's not an answer."

"I enjoy watching you warmbloods go on your way to work and then come home. The looks on your faces, the differences in how you carry yourselves ... I can tell if you've had good days or bad. I can tell if you have plans, or if you were just going to stay home for the evening. While the restaurant and my apartment were coming together, it was a nice way to begin or end the day." I didn't say that it hadn't become a regular occurrence until I'd begun to see her every day. "Then, of course, I must keep my two elder ladies busy praying for me."

"Ah, I see. Why here?"

"Like you, I like the area. Uptown is too stuffy."

"Okay, why else?"

"It's disconcerting when you do that," I said.

She rose and took the dishes over to the sink. "Do what?"

"See through my non-answers." Most people didn't. It reminded me of my adopted *eomeoni*. I could hide nothing from her.

She laughed and came back to the table. I pulled her back onto my lap. "I'm observant."

"The bluebloods think they're slumming when they come downtown. I have made them think my establishment is so exclusive that we will give them a private place to do all their dirty dealings—that they're safe. They grew indolent and arrogant while I was away. The restaurant is not for them. It's for me to learn their secrets and take back what was lost."

"You'll use the information against them?"

"If need be, absolutely."

Her heartbeat sped up, but not in fear. I couldn't begin to think what was going through her head. "Why were you away?" Was the only thing she asked.

"Our father had business for me. He also wanted to test Phillip. My brother failed that test." An understatement. My brother is a complete fuck up, and he went a long way to destroy what I'd built in this city and on this coast. "He went through a lot of money and a lot of drugs. But he damaged our standing as a family and as a business entity. The restaurant is my way of trying to regain ground. Well, it's one way. Right now, the place is hot and so it serves my needs quite well. People are very careless when they think no one is listening."

"So, while the right hand gives, the left takes," she said.

"Yes. Very astute. They think they're getting something, but they're giving me ammunition."

"I want to say eat the rich, but you're also rich."

"Yes, I am. But they have lost respect and fear of me. This is about power and control. Had I been here, this whole thing with your father would never have happened, and Jennings and Deveraux would be dead already."

She twisted around and straddled me. "That is positively primitive, yet it's also super-hot. I am not sure where my head is at now that I feel that way."

"Maybe," I said, opening her robe and cupping her pussy. "You like power. Maybe it excites you and feeds that anger of yours. Because now you've met someone from whom you don't have to hide it." Her eyes widened. "I strike a nerve?"

"You did," she said, undoing my pants. "But I want to point out it goes both ways." She pulled my cock out and stroked it.

"Oh?" I pushed her robe off her shoulders. "Is that so, little flower?"

"It is." She lifted herself, and I helped guide her right over my cock. In one swift movement, I was inside her. She arched her back, riding me as her nails dug into my chest.

I gripped her hips but let her set the rhythm. It was hard not to stop and watch her as she moved on me. She took one hand from my shoulder and played with her clit. I groaned. "You are so fucking beautiful," I whispered.

She kissed me. It was hard and possessive. Her tongue swept into my mouth, and I sucked on it as she moved faster on me, moving towards her orgasm. I wound one hand around her hair and kept our mouths locked in a kiss.

She broke me apart and put me back together at the same time. Tongues and teeth crashed into each other as if we couldn't get enough of each other. And the truth was, we couldn't.

She arched and groaned as she bucked and came. She kept riding me, driving me to my own. I came quickly, my mouth back on hers for another bruising kiss.

When we finally pulled apart, she did the damnedest thing. She leaned down and placed a soft kiss on the bare skin over my heart. Quite suddenly, I was undone.

ABIGAIL

Anderson left early the next morning while it was still dark, insisting he had to see his ladies off to the church. But he left Soames and Keith outside my apartment to guard me. I didn't think it was necessary, but he insisted anyone with half a brain could get past the doorman.

Originally, I hadn't wanted them in my apartment, but I had two other neighbors on the floor who would wonder what two vampires were doing camped in the hallway. So, I had them come in and sit in the living room while I worked in my office. I called in sick but wanted to gather and organize information. Anderson's second, Jack, called me that morning, and we had a long discussion about what he and I needed.

By early afternoon, I not only had all the finances for my boss, Jennings, and Miranda Summers, I had them for the entire board of mine and my father's companies. Jack was efficient, and I appreciated that. I started with the people I didn't think were involved and steadily crossed most off my list. A few had odd discrepancies, which may or may not be connected, but they needed closer scrutiny. When I got to the last of those, something caught my eye. A board member for Allied Tech was my uncle's brother-in-law. And his finances were odd.

I sighed and called Jack. "What may I do for you, Miss Eastman?"

"Firstly, you can call me Abigail."

"Oh no, I don't think so," he sounded taken aback.

"You know it's *my* name. You do not need Anderson's okay for this."

"As you say, Miss Eastman."

I sighed. "Fine," I said. I would discuss that with Anderson later. "I need to get the finances for an Evan Woodman, please? For the last several years."

"A moment, please," I could hear him typing. "Check your email."

"You already pulled his information for Anderson, didn't you?"

"I can neither confirm nor deny this,"

"You don't need to confirm it. There'd be no other reason you'd have my uncle's information readily at hand. Thank you, Jack."

"Most welcome, Miss Eastman."

Uncle Evan's finances were, in a word, chaos. He and the company hemorrhaged money for years. He had come close to ruin, but the company saw an odd influx of cash three years ago. There had also been a huge deposit right before my dad was arrested. And then a handful of payouts for the next six months to a company that rang a bell, but I couldn't place it. And those payouts had an odd paper trail. In the last three months, another company had made payments into my uncle's company. It was all odd, convoluted, and very sloppy.

It would likely take no time at all for Anderson to ruin him if he chose to do so. Evan's company was doing better but was a house of cards. I wanted to feel something about this: sympathy, compassion, empathy. But I felt nothing. This man had turned his back on my mother—more than once. We had seen him a few times, and he always ignored her, going so far as to physically turn his back on her. Each time, I remembered how her face crumpled at the slight. How hurt she had looked. How upset she'd be for days afterward.

I did feel something, actually. It was rage.

ANDERSON

I spent a good deal of Monday discovering everything I could about Abigail's grandparents and uncle. A cursory glance told me they were definitely assholes. Tight-assed and blue-blooded in the worst way. I'd seen it hundreds of times over my lifetime. They didn't like anyone outside of their small circle. They had wanted Abigail's mother, Beverly, to marry someone else. Someone of their choosing. But she'd fallen in love with Jacob Eastman and would not be deterred.

Abigail had been right. They issued an ultimatum, and Beverly walked away. They cut her off emotionally and tried to cut her off financially, but they couldn't do anything about Beverly's trust fund. Once she'd come of age, she ended the trust and used the money to start one for her daughter. I had learned all of this from a childhood friend of Beverly's, who was more than happy to gossip with me.

Beverly tried to connect with her parents every so often throughout the years to no avail. She attended both their funerals, but her brother ignored her and even tried to get her kicked out of her mother's funeral. But it was more insidious than that. Beverly's father had done what he could to try and ruin Jacob's career. When he died, her uncle picked up the mantle. Jacob was well respected, so nothing touched him, but the three men were playing the long game.

I could sit here and say I wasn't going to ruin Evan Woodman, but it would be a lie. I could also try and convince myself I wouldn't end his pathetic existence at some point. That would also be a lie. My phone rang.

"Jack?"

"Miss Eastman has requested Evan Woodman's financials. I do not know why."

"Interesting. You did provide them?"

"Of course I did." He sounded affronted.

"She must have found some connection. Woodman is involved in this. I am sure of it."

"Quite possibly," Jack said. "I've set up meetings with both CEOs for you."

"Thank you," I said. "What was their reaction?"

"Fear. They think you're going to take over their companies.

"They'll be lucky if *all* I do is take over their companies. Does it seem like they know what's going on?"

"May I be honest?"

"You need never ask that," I replied.

"If either of those men knew what's happening, I would be surprised. They're old, and they're old money. They inherited these companies and deal with them minimally. The board does the hiring and firing of upper management."

"At a minimum, both boards will need to be replaced."

"Agreed. The CEOs shrug and play golf with the other lazy bastards who have too much money and too little time."

"You don't think much of the wealthy, do you?"

"Not true," Jack answered. "I think well of those who do the work. The ones who don't let their brains atrophy and have their staff do everything while they take all the credit. Like you, Anderson. You got back and went to work fixing your brother's mess. You didn't need to; it's not like you needed the money."

Jack surprised me. He was not an effusive man, and this speech was a lot for him. "I need control," I answered. And let's face it, I liked the power. My *abeoji*, the man who sired me, had taught me power and control were important, but the goal was to take care of the people who counted on you and to excise those that were a cancer. I tried to do that. I was fine with being feared; it was preferable in most cases. I mete out punishment when necessary. If you were a person that feared me, it was likely because you had done something to make me angry.

"Yes, you do." Jack was always honest with me. "But you're not taking over the mom-and-pop stores or small companies. They may ask for your help, but you don't run them down." Jack was thinking of his sister. She ran a small business that had been the target of harassment and sabotage. Jack came to me and asked for my assistance. I saw how smart and tough he was and hired him immediately.

"I have, though, in the past. It is not something I am proud of. And the fact the one thing my brother was doing was ruining small businesses still pisses me off." And I was still trying to fix that, but trust had been broken. I wanted to kill the little shit for that alone.

"The past is not now. Hopefully, your brother will learn."

"With luck. But we've strayed from the topic."

"We have. So, the meetings are going to be at the restaurant. I thought it best they are not at their offices or homes."

"Agreed. I want these on my turf. What do we have from Deveraux or Jennings?"

"Silence."

"I don't like it. We need to find out what's going on and close the gaps on this."

"Already on it. I can report Deveraux could not find an emergency dentist yesterday. As a matter of fact, he could not get an appointment until tomorrow morning. Such a shame," Jack snickered.

"Ah, it is good to be me," I laughed. It was petty of me to ensure he didn't get a dentist appointment, and I can live with that. I've done worse.

"I can have Tim send you an audio file of the phone calls to different dentists if you'd like."

"I should not want that, but I do. Thank you. When are the meetings?"

"Allied Tech is tomorrow's lunch. Power Dynamics is drinks at six."

"Wonderful. Thank you, Jack."

Jack and I discussed other business, and then I headed over to Abigail's. Soames let me in. "How are things here?"

"Fine." Soames shrugged. "She's been holed up in her office all day. She's come out a few times to grab a coffee, food, or to check on us."

"Check on you?"

Keith nodded. "To make sure we're doing okay and if we need anything." I gave him a look. "Really, Sir. She's very considerate."

"It's true. She is." Soames paused. "I am not sure she's had enough food today, though."

"I think she was very focused on what she was doing," Keith said.

"Agreed," said Soames. "Even with that, she could have eaten more." I smiled at her. "What? I am telling you what I've seen."

"Thank you, both. You can go now. You have the evening off."

"Oh, that's lovely then, boss. Thanks." Keith smiled at me. He had been young when turned, not by my hand—or fangs—so he'd always be boyishly good-looking. Seventy-five years as a vampire, and his personality hadn't changed much. Neither had Soames'. That's why I put them together.

I locked the door and walked down the hallway, looking for Abigail's office. I could smell her, but it was soft. I eased open a door and saw her curled in an oversized chair in the corner. She had a soft blanket over her and was snoring softly. She was adorable, and a vice squeezed my heart for a moment. I rubbed that spot and tried to ignore it. It had only been a few days. There was no need for this.

I walked over to the chair and lifted her gently. I thought she'd wake, but she curled into me, and that vice got tighter. I took off my shoes, having forgotten to remove them at the door, and settled onto the chair with her on my lap. I put my feet on the ottoman and held her while she napped.

I let my thoughts wander while Abigail burrowed further into me. She wrapped her arms around my waist and sighed, then settled. I looked around the room and smiled. There were family photos all over the place and giant photo prints of different locations on the wall. I recognized Holyrood Palace, the Eiffel Tower, and Kinkakuji Temple in Kyoto, to name a few. I remembered when that was built. My father and I happened to be in Japan at the time. It seemed Abigail liked to take pictures of places she'd been and surround herself with them.

I also spied a small fridge under her desk. Chances are she had snacks in there, as well as beverages. I kissed her head and closed my eyes, surprised at how peaceful I felt with her.

I sighed quietly. It was silly to try and fool myself. I was developing feelings for this woman and probably had been since I first saw her.

The problem was, for the first time in centuries, I had no idea what to do about it. I had spent several lifetimes never getting too close to humans, especially women. But Abigail was different. I felt different with her.

I was flummoxed. But while thinking about the puzzle that was Abigail, I did the most unexpected thing ... I relaxed and fell asleep.

***

I woke from my unexpected nap when Abigail stirred. I hadn't meant to fall asleep. This was one more way I was under her spell. I had spent the night last night, another anomaly, though I hadn't slept.

"Nice nap, little flower?" I asked her.

"Yes," she answered, her voice husky. "You?"

"Actually, yes."

"I'm glad," She stretched, showing a bit of her stomach as the top she had on rode up. "I like this outfit. It's soft, like you." I ran my hand down her side, and she shivered.

"It's sweats and a cropped hoodie," she answered, blushing a little. A blush that covered her body.

"In cashmere?" I asked.

"I admit, I am a sucker for soft things," she said. "Except when I'm not." She waggled her brows at me, and I had to laugh. My *abeoji* had once told me a woman who can please your body was nice, but a woman who could hold your mind and make you laugh was what you really wanted. That was a woman you held onto at all costs. He had loved my *eomeoni* very much, and it had almost destroyed him when she had passed. She was human and hadn't wanted to become a vampire, though she loved my father. I considered her a mother more than the woman who had borne me.

Abigail made me feel good in both body and mind. I loved making her come, but I also wanted to make her smile and laugh. It's annoying when your parents are right, even when you are a vampire.

I kissed her softly, and she looked at me in surprise and wonder.

In stories, what happened when the villain began to fall in love?

ABIGAIL

Something was going on in Anderson's head, and I had no idea what it could be. "You're probably not hungry, but I could eat."

"Soames and Keith said you didn't eat much today."

I frowned. "Do you have them keeping tabs on me?"

"Hardly," he replied. "They offered the information freely. I suspect they were concerned."

"I highly doubt Soames was concerned."

"You'd be surprised." He paused. "Abigail, you need to eat."

I sighed and stood, immediately missing the heat and comfort of him. I walked over to my mini-fridge and opened it. "As you can see, snacks. Yogurt, cheese, hardboiled eggs. And water." I closed the fridge and pointed to a jar. "Almonds." He didn't need to know about the chocolate stash. "I like to eat, but I also tend to get hyper-focused when working on challenging or interesting problems. I keep snacks handy."

Anderson stood. "I am not trying to manage you, Abigail."

"Aren't you?" I asked. "You're used to managing people."

"Has it occurred to you I want you to eat so you do not fall ill?"

I blinked. "No, it hadn't occurred to me. We haven't known each other for long," I offered by way of both explanation and apology.

"That's fair, and yes, I am used to managing people. But, Abigail, if you're not taking care of yourself, I will say something. I do not want you to fall ill. Additionally, you need to be well for what we're doing here. It takes energy and stamina."

I moved to stand in front of him. "What *are* we doing here?" I looked at him, not sure how I meant this question.

He looked at me like he wanted to say something, then his gaze shuttered. He took a deep breath and spoke. . "We are trying to free your father by exposing both Jennings and Deveraux."

"With the side bonus of ruining my uncle?"

"Yes. I am not going to just ruin him, little flower. I am going to annihilate him."

"Well, I think I can help with that." I started toward the kitchen, once again with Anderson following me. The discussion of my eating habits had annoyed me some, and now I was feeling out of sorts.

"I'm all ears," he purred behind me.

"Carbonara," I said.

"That's going to help me ruin your uncle?"

"No, it's what we're having for dinner." As I cooked, I told him what I'd discovered that day. "I only know it's his brother-in-law because when I was fourteen, I got obsessed with finding out everything about my uncle."

"Why?" Anderson asked, pouring me wine.

I made a face. "I was going to ruin him."

"As a teenager?"

"Yes. I know absolutely crazy that sounds. But, my grandmother had just died, and he ignored my mother at the funeral. He sent his brother-in-law over to try and convince my mom to leave. It was the only time I saw my father angry. Even then, he was very calm."

"You stayed," he guessed.

"We stayed. I haven't discounted the possibility that someone on the board at my company is connected to Uncle Evan."

"Why is that?"

"The money in, the money out, and then the money back in again. It's sloppy. There are three holding companies involved. I've figured out that much. I need to figure out who they belong to." I got the pasta out of the pot, adding the other ingredients for the carbonara. I found cooking centered me and today was no exception. Anderson watched for a few minutes.

"You have a theory?" he finally asked.

"I do. But I am not saying anything yet."

"What do you need from me?"

I put the pasta into bowls and carried them to the table. He followed with the wine. I set the bowls down, and we sat. "I could use a computer hacker," I replied half-jokingly.

"Done. Send all the information to Jack, and he'll put you in contact with someone."

"Just like that?" I asked.

"Just like that, Abigail."

I nodded. It made sense he had hackers. "Thank you. I have to work tomorrow, but I will send Jack what I need before the day begins."

"You are working from home, yes?" I nodded. "Good."

"I am a bit nervous about Deveraux and how he'll be."

"He'll be seeing a dentist first thing in the morning. I wouldn't expect to hear from him until later in the day." He smiled wolfishly.

"I'm surprised he couldn't get an appointment before this." I looked at Anderson, who just shrugged. "Ah, I see. I had no idea you had an in with dentists."

"I have my ways. In the spirit of collaboration, I have meetings with both CEOs tomorrow."

"Useless men," I said. "Old money who inherited the companies. They won't know anything."

"Jack said much the same. But that suits my needs fine. They're weak, and I can use weak to my advantage."

"What are you planning to do?" I asked, taking a bite of pasta. Carbonara was a comfort meal for me, and between it, the wine, and Anderson's presence, I was less stressed than I had been all day. I had been upset at Anderson's nagging me about eating again, but maybe he had a point. My father's arrest and trial had thrown our lives into disarray, and I had been having trouble getting back into my routine. Cooking and eating this meal had settled me.

"I am planning to clean house. And if they won't fall in line, they will find themselves with one less asset."

"Why are you doing this?"

"I thought we covered this."

"Not really. Do you help all the women you fuck?"

He stared at me for a moment. "No, I don't. Just you. I like puzzles. This is a puzzle."

"I see," I said, taking our plates to the sink. "Of course."

He growled. "Fuck, Abigail! What do you want from me?"

"I ... I don't know! It's been four fucking days! I have no idea what the hell is wrong with me. I am sorry." I covered my face with my hands. This was embarrassing.

His arms came around, pulling me into an embrace. "It's been a year and four days. A year of both of us thinking about each other, and then four days of intense intimacy and plots to have your father acquitted and freed from prison. You are frustrated and tired. You wonder if I have ulterior motives. I always have ulterior motives, Abigail. In this case, it furthers my plans to take back my city. I am confident you have realized this. But it's not my primary motivation."

"No?" I asked against his chest.

"No, little flower. I don't like what was done to you or your father by these people. You're also wondering if you can trust me. You can. But I am not a man used to sharing his work. This is new territory, and I am doing my best."

"Same," I replied. "And I do trust you."

"I'm glad. Abigail ..."

"At this point, you can call me Abbie."

"Abbie, I don't have what you would call friends. I have allies or employees." I stiffened a little, and he rubbed my back. "I don't let people close to me. I don't stay the night. I don't sit in kitchens while women cook for me. It's too intimate. I don't nap with women, and I sure as shit do not get involved in their lives. Until you. So yes, we are fucking, but we are also more than that. What that thing is, I have no idea. Do you?"

I shook my head. "I don't." But I had a good idea why I felt this way. I didn't want to face it yet. I wasn't ready. And the timing felt wrong.

"Then we'll figure this out together, free your dad and ruin some people."

"Just ruin?" I asked.

"No, but that will only be me." He paused. "And that is something you are going to have to think about. You will need to decide if the violence that lives in me is acceptable to you."

I suspected I knew the answer to that too. And I wasn't ready to face that either. "I know," was my only reply.

"You need to get to bed early, Abbie."

I looked at him. "Oh?"

"That's not what I meant," he said.

"I know," I said, but my hands wandered.

Anderson picked me up, and I wrapped my legs around his waist. "Well, I've never fucked anyone to sleep before, but now seems a good time to start."

***

It was a long week. Deveraux spent it trying to undermine or humiliate me during meetings. Additionally, he or someone else tried to mess with my work, change my numbers. Since my father's arrest, I have added encryption to all my files. If you weren't me, you couldn't change them. Didn't stop them from trying. Deveraux made sly references to Anderson in every meeting while I ignored them and stayed calm. But it wore on me and I was exhausted by the end of each day.

The one good thing was connecting with Anderson's hacker. Melanie, or Mel as they asked to be called, was a whirlwind. They talked quickly and had bright blue hair and piercings along both ears. They were human, not a vampire, and we liked each other immediately.

It took them a couple of days to unravel all the knots. "It's not that they were good knots," they said. "There was a lot of them. This is how people hide things when they don't know what the fuck they're doing. Simple is best. People overlook the simple shit all the time. They don't think it can possibly be anything because it's too simple." They peered at me through the computer camera. "But the truth is, the simple stuff is always something. It's just that no one expects simple."

"Do you think they hired someone or set it up themselves?" I asked, fascinated.

"Probably themselves. This is sloppy. My niece can do better than this." They found a series of fake holding companies and offshore accounts. Mel confirmed all the players and how they connected. It was galling and disappointing but hardly surprising.

"Anything about who's been trying to change my files?" I asked.

"Yup. Deveraux and Summers. Summers was a lot smarter about it. Deveraux is a fucking moron. But your encryption skills are good. You were trained well. I can add a couple more fail-safes if you'd like."

"I would love that, thank you! And thank you for all of this!"

"Most welcome. I live for this shit." They paused a moment. "So, Anderson is paying me for this job, but I was wondering if you might be willing to look at my finances. I can break into any computer and remember PI up to 15 digits, but balancing my books makes me insane. I don't know what's an asset or what's an expense half the time."

"Sure," I said. "Send it all to me. I started in tax accounting, and I can probably help streamline your process." I loved running numbers and making columns add up. And I loved helping people with their money and working with smaller businesses. It's honestly what I'd rather be doing. And once this whole thing was over, I'd think about making that a reality.

"Cool! It's a bit of a mess since I have a legit business helping companies with their online security." They chuckled. "I'd like to try and find a way to marry that business with this business."

"I should be able to help with that."

"Great! I will shoot it right over to you! Thanks!"

Mel had definitely been the highlight of the week thus far.

I'd barely seen Anderson after Monday night, and it made me irritable. At some point on Thursday, I had to admit the truth: I was falling in love with a vampire after barely a week of knowing him. And not just any old vampire, a vampire known for being blood thirsty. And that didn't even bother me. Not even a little bit. Maybe it would when I saw him in action. He was right when he suggested I liked not hiding my anger anymore. He understood and accepted it. Hell, the scent of my anger was a turn-on for him. Shit like that can turn a girl's head.

And while I liked Soames and Keith, I didn't always like having them underfoot. I refused to sleep with anyone else in the apartment, so Anderson got creative with my overnight security—something else I didn't love, and we'd argued over the phone. Ultimately, he made it clear he was doing it anyway, and there wasn't much I could do. Then, when I'd been about to blow up, he said he'd feel better knowing I was safe. If he couldn't be here, he needed to know no harm would come to me. I couldn't say no after that. And now, I was pretty sure I had vampires hanging out on the window ledges outside my apartment.

I called to tell him I had information from Mel but wanted to see him in person to relay it. Mostly, I wanted to see him.

"Well done, little flower. Why don't you come over tomorrow night for dinner? We can have drinks with Jack beforehand and share all our information."

"Fine. The restaurant?"

"No, my apartment. Stay the night with me, Abbie." His voice was a husky whisper.

"Oh," I said. "I'd love that." That was a surprise, but a nice one.

"Good. I've missed you, and I have plans for you." He mentioned he had business to take care of for his father this week, and it had kept us apart.

"And what do these plans involve?"

"You naked in my bed, for starters," came the reply.

"I'll be ready," I said, trying not to melt.

"Good, see you then."

II walked over to my bedroom closet and opened it. I was lucky enough to have a walk-in closet. I wanted something that would knock Anderson's socks off. I had bought several sexy little numbers for absolutely no reason other than they made me happy, and I was convinced one of them would do the trick. I smiled and pulled one out. Yup, this would make his eyes melt, but other parts hard, hopefully. I smiled. Tomorrow could not come soon enough.

ANDERSON

The week was long and annoying. I barely saw Abbie, and that pissed me off. She was also having a shit week but wasn't saying anything. Based on what I heard from Deveraux's calls about how he was treating her, he's lucky I didn't go over there and rip his fucking head off.

I opted to meet both CEOs at my office upstairs from the restaurant together. Addison Reames and Jackson Harlow were two of the most useless people I'd ever met. They had both virtually ceded control of their companies to their CFOs, out of sheer laziness. They couldn't give a fuck. But each of them had adult children who were more than capable and very interested in running the companies. They were hungry for it and were more than willing to throw in with me and do what I told them to.

I was not an idiot. At some point, they'd try and test me. For now, Natalie Reames and Jackson Harlow Jr. suited my needs. The two old men blustered about it, but I told them I'd destroy them if they butted in further. They'd retire when I told them to, and they would decline positions on the board of directors. I'd be cherry-picking new board members myself when the time came.

I listened to a good deal of audio from Deveraux, Jennings, and Summers and read several emails and texts, in between handling some business for my father. Most of them did not say much of anything, and no one mentioned or implicated Evan Woodman. Mostly they complained and showboated. It was disgusting. But it made me suspicious.

Listening to Miranda Summers talk about Abbie made me so angry I put my fist through a wall.

"That little Eastman bitch thinks she has us figured out, that she's smarter than us."

"She's got Anderson Jeon in her pocket now, though." This was Deveraux, the king of the whiners.

"Anderson likes a good piece of ass," Jennings snorted. "He's got a reputation. He'll get bored of her. Little tight-ass that she is." I didn't think I had a reputation. I was generally discreet. That said, Abbie's ass was not Jennings's business.

Summers laughed. "Correct. It won't last. She's confided in me that none of her relationships have. I know so much to manipulate her with. She's trash. Her family is trash." I don't like hurting women, but Summers tested my limits.

"We may have to kill her," Jennings said. "I don't think she'll be stopped. Maybe Jeon will back off once she's out of the picture."

I snorted. If something happened to Abigail, I would not back off. I had to wonder at their stupidity and arrogance. If listening to their conversations told me anything, it was that thought they were better than everyone else. The way they dissected people and treated those around was arrogant and cruel. Jacob discovered what they were doing, so they stopped him. But they got cocky and this made them sloppy. They counted on people not taking a deeper look because of who they were. It was going to be a joy taking them down.

"I want her before you kill her," Deveraux said. "She always thought she was too good for me."

"Fine," said Jennings. "You can have her. I don't care."

My eyes narrowed. None of them would ever touch her. If they tried, I would torture them for as long as it took to drive them insane from the pain. I would relish every scream I wrung from them. Every drop of their blood would be a victory. They'd wish for death, but it would be a long time coming.

Suddenly, I knew what happened to the villain when he fell in love. He became the man who burned the world down to keep her safe.

ABIGAIL

Anderson came and picked me up himself on Friday. "Abigail, why are you wearing that trench coat? I swear I will burn it." He looked aggrieved at the mere sight of it.

I laughed. "Because what's under it is a surprise. And I want to torture you a little."

"You have no other coats or jackets?"

"I do. But I know how you love this one." I kissed him on the cheek.

He sighed. "This had better be worth it."

"It is!" We traveled back to his apartment. The building had four stories. Two belonged to the restaurant. We were having drinks on the third floor, where Anderson had some conference and reception areas, as well as a lounge.

"Coat off, now. I cannot bear looking at it any longer."

I laughed and removed my jacket. I was wearing a tight-fitting corset dress in a deep blue with a pair of silver strappy sandals. To say my assets were on display would be an understatement. Anderson stared at me, not saying anything.

"What's wrong? Say something! Do you hate it?" I was worried now. He was staring, and I couldn't figure out the look on his face.

My words snapped him out of his thoughts. "Oh no, little flower. I like it very much. I am going to have trouble not tearing it off you." He pulled me to him and put both hands on my rear. "But Jack is coming for a drink to discuss business, so that will have to wait." He sucked my bottom lip into his mouth, and I steadied myself on his shoulders.

"Glad you like it," I said a little breathlessly.

"I adore it. You are very much on display, though."

"Yes," I said. "I am." I winked at him, and he growled at me. I laughed.

Someone cleared their throat from the door. "Ah, Jack. Punctual as usual. Thank you for coming."

Jack Atkinson was a handful of inches shorter than Anderson but stocky. His dark hair was cut short, and I could believe he used to be a marine. "It's no problem, Anderson. Miss Eastman, it's a pleasure to meet you in person."

I put my hand out, and he shook it. "It's Abigail. Please, Jack."

"Miss Eastman ..."

"I will call you by your last name if you don't stop it," I said.

"Jack," laughed Anderson. "Call the woman by her first name."

"Oh, well, fine then. Nice to meet you, Abigail."

"Wonderful. Now that the pleasantries are out of the way, drinks?" Anderson asked.

"Yes," I replied. "It's been that kind of week."

"Agreed," said Jack. "I can make drinks."

"No," said Anderson. "I will make them. The usual?" Jack nodded. "Abbie, what about you?"

"What's Jack's usual?" I asked.

"Old Fashioned," responded Jack.

"Oh, nice! I'll have the same."

"Coming up! Please have a seat," Anderson said, getting to work on the drinks.

Jack and I sat and made small talk. His phone pinged, and he frowned, looking at it. "Anything wrong?" I asked.

"Not really. My sister texted me her bookkeeper quit, and she can't figure out what he did to her accounts."

"Oh, have her send me her stuff. I'll take a look."

Jack looked horrified. "Oh, I don't want to impose. You have a lot going on."

"I don't mind. I love doing that kind of work. It's like a puzzle. I like puzzles."

Anderson's head shot up at my words, and Jack laughed. "Yeah, you two are a good match," he said. "Thank you. I'll give my sister your email."

I looked at Anderson. "You like puzzles? He nodded. "That makes sense." I couldn't picture us working on a jigsaw puzzle like I used to do with Dad, but he liked figuring things out the same way I did. I found that comforting.

Anderson brought over our drinks and took a seat. "I have always liked puzzles since I was a small boy in Korea. Now, the puzzles are bigger, but I enjoy figuring things out, having them make sense."

"Was I a puzzle to you?" I asked.

"Yes. And I was one for you," he replied, sipping his drink. "Okay, do you want to go first, or should we?"

"Oh, let me," I replied. "Damn, this drink is amazing." I took another sip. "Mel is amazing, and they managed to figure out all the players. There's one holding company that started the whole thing. That person had the initial plan. They found the other players, and it went from there."

"You know who started this, don't you?" Anderson asked.

"I do. And you either suspect the same person or know it's them—my uncle Evan. He started this whole thing to destroy my father. And now, probably me as well."

Anderson nodded. "We didn't know for sure, but we did suspect him."

Jack cleared his throat. "I come bearing a piece of information of my own. I learned from a bartender friend that Evan Woodman and Miranda Summers have been having an affair for years."

I blinked at him. "Miranda used to tell me about the man she was seeing. She said it needed to be a secret because he was married—something I am against—but he was powerful and smart. And a dynamo in bed." I put my hand to my mouth. "Oh, god, I want to throw up."

Anderson took my hand and kissed my knuckles. "I cannot blame you. She was telling you all of this as a perverse joke." Anderson relayed the conversations he had listened to, and I got angrier, which was better than nauseated.

Jack took in Anderson holding my hand but said nothing, only smiling slightly.

I sipped my drink. "So, Miranda's illegal holding company funneled in a sizeable amount of money to my uncle right when he needed it. As I am sure you saw, the company was close to going under."

Anderson nodded. "Woodman concocts this plan, for some reason, to ruin your father, and goes to Miranda with it. She brings in Deveraux and Jennings."

"Right, that's how I think it went as well. She told them they could get rid of the Eastmans for good, but it would take money. They paid her, and she paid Woodman, helping keep the company afloat. He then ensured his brother-in-law was on the board of Allied Tech."

"Pretty ballsy move when you're cheating on the man's sister," Jack said.

"Indeed," Anderson replied. "So, the payments were to his brother-in-law?"

I nodded. "Yes. The company was familiar to me, but I couldn't place why. Once I knew it was a Wilbur holding company, a legal one, I figured it out. My dad used to run audits on all the new board members. He usually asked me to check his numbers. Mart Wilbur's numbers were not bad, but odd. It was probably that first payment or two."

"Jennings wasn't going to check it out because he knew what the payments were," Jack said.

"Which makes sense in hindsight. After Dad went to jail, Uncle Evan got the last payment. A job well done." My tone was bitter.

"He'll pay, Abbie. All of them will pay. I promise you," Anderson's voice was hard.

"I believe you," I said. We looked at each other for a long moment until Jack cleared his throat.

"I don't understand why Woodman did this," Anderson mused. "You don't talk to each other. He's ignored you for years. Deveraux or Jennings instigating this would have made more sense."

"I agree. I am going to visit my dad on Sunday. I'll ask him if he knows why."

"I'll take you," Anderson said.

"That's not necessary." I frowned at him.

"I want to. Unless you don't want him to know you're seeing a vampire."

I gaped at him. "That's ridiculous!"

"Then what is the problem?" Anderson asked coolly.

"There isn't one. Visiting a prison is not something people want to do." It was a serious step when I didn't know where this relationship was going. It unnerved me, especially considering what I was thinking about doing later.

"You're going, and I'm going. I'd like to meet your father." He squeezed my hand. "No matter what, this ends soon."

We all spoke for a little longer, Anderson told me what had gone on with the CEO meeting, and Jack added a few other details until he stood. "Well, this has been enlightening, but I am going to my sister's for dinner. So, I need to get going." I was pretty sure the enlightening comment was about me and Anderson and not so much about the situation. He seemed to have settled his mind where it concerned Anderson and myself.

Anderson and I went to his apartment, slipping our shoes off in the entryway. It was different from what I expected. It was a mix of contemporary design and a traditional Hanok-style home. "What do you think?" he asked. He sounded a little nervous.

I did a 180 and smiled at him. "This is lovely. Not what I expected, but it suits you. You incorporated a traditional Korean home into your private space."

He wrapped his arms around me from behind, resting his head on mine. "It connects me to my home and my father."

"Your vampire father?" I asked.

"Yes. I remember my human parents, but it was not a good childhood."

"I'm sorry," I said quietly.

"No matter," he said. "I'm glad you like it. You're the first person I've brought here."

"You're joking! I'm the first?" I turned to him, wanting to see his eyes.

He looked down at me. "No joke, little flower. You are the first person I've had in this space. And you will likely be the only person I will ever allow here."

"What about other women you've ..."

"There is a bedroom downstairs. Right off the area we had drinks in. That's a social space but not my sanctuary. If I am honest, I don't think anyone ever noticed."

"I would have," I said softly.

"Yes, you would have." He kissed the top of my head.

I blew out my breath. I had been warring with myself all day about this, but I was going to dive in feet first and hope for the best. "I'm honored you're sharing your home with me. And I have something I want to say to you." I don't think I would be doing this if we had been in that room downstairs.

He gave me a soft kiss. "Go on," he said. He looked almost ... hopeful. And that gave me the courage to forge ahead with this.

"We've only been together a week, and I have no business saying this to you, but I am going to anyway. You told me I needed to decide how I felt about certain things, namely your violent nature. I do not think you have one. I believe you may, and can, and will, commit violent acts when necessary. But your nature is not one of violence. Your home tells me that. I am fine with who you are and what you need to do sometimes. I love you."

He blinked at me. "What did you say, Abigail?"

"I said I loved you. I don't know that I've been in love before, or if this is how you do it ..." I never finished my sentence because he kissed me quite thoroughly.

"I take it," —I said when we pulled apart— "that is not an unpleasant notion." I didn't care if he said it back. Well, that's not true; I did. But I didn't expect it. So, his next words shocked me.

"Little flower, I love you as well. I loved you before I had even spoken to you."

"Oh wow, I had not expected that. But I am glad." We stood there for a while, holding each other, and kissing occasionally.

"Are you hungry?" he finally asked.

"Not for food," came my reply.

He pulled back. "We can eat later, then." He bit his lip, looking a little unsure.

"What's wrong?"

"Well, I had planned something for tonight, but I am rethinking."

"What did you have planned?" He pulled me to him, running his hands underneath my dress. His hand pulled my thong aside as he slid his fingers into the crease and ran along the hole.

"Oh," I said. "I see. No, I think this is a good plan we should continue with."

"Are you sure?"

"Yes. I am not sure why admitting we loved each other would change that plan."

"It doesn't seem romantic," he said, shrugging. "My father would want me to do something romantic."

"Helping free my father from jail is pretty romantic. If being in love means you won't continue fucking me as you have been, we should rethink this." I kissed the tip of his nose.

He laughed. "I must admit, this love thing is a bit new to me."

"In twelve hundred years, you've not been in love?" I thought of the blank spot of skin over his heart.

"No. I do not believe so. I've never let someone get this close to me before."

"That makes two of us, then." I ran my hands over his rear end and squeezed. "We'll figure it out as we go along. But for now, I say we move ahead with butt sex."

Anderson threw back his head and laughed at this. The best sound there was. "Is that new to you?" he asked.

I shook my head. "Sorry, you will not be the first."

"But I will be the last," he said emphatically. "Who was it?" I gave him a look. "I am not going to go find them. Probably."

"Yes, you will be the last. He was someone I had been with for a year. He wanted to try it, and I was amenable. He also wanted a threesome, but we could not agree on the shape it should take."

"Meaning what?"

"He wanted another woman. I wanted another man." I shrugged. "In the end, it didn't matter because he was cheating on me with the woman he wanted the threesome with."

"Perhaps I should pay this man a visit."

"If he hadn't cheated on me, I may still be with him today, and we wouldn't be here now."

"You make a fair point."

"I thought you might see it my way. Now, I do expect my quota of orgasms, though."

He swung me into his arms easily. I liked vampire strength. "Naturally. I need to peel that dress off you."

"I am glad you liked the dress," I said.

"I do. Have you more like it?" We walked into his bedroom, a mix of contemporary and Korean. "I think I would enjoy that."

"I do. I have a bevy of sexy dresses in my closet. Just in case I met a sexy vampire."

"Lucky you, then." He lowered his head and ran his tongue across the tops of my breasts while he unzipped the dress. It fell away, leaving me there in my thong. He fell to his knees and took one nipple in his mouth while playing with the other. I put my hands in his hair to keep my balance.

"Anderson," I said breathlessly. "Jesus, that feels good."

"I know," he smirked.

"You are a wicked man," I laughed.

"Mmm," he said against my breast. He bit gently, and I bucked against him, so he bit again but harder. I moaned. "You are a feast for the senses."

He pulled my thong down and nudged my legs apart. He put his mouth on my clit and sucked as his fingers made their way to my ass. He rubbed me back there before pulling back.

"Hold a moment," he said.

"What? Where are you going? And why are you still wearing so many clothes?"

He laughed. "How could I do anything *but* love you?" he asked. "I am going to get some oil."

"Oh, fine. Come back with less clothing on."

He was gone for a minute and came back shirtless, carrying something in his hand. He pulled me to him and kissed me deeply. "Better?" he asked.

"Yes, but you could still lose the pants." I could look at him naked all day long and never get bored. It wasn't just the tattoos; all that lean muscle was such a lovely package.

"I will, never fear." He dropped back to his knees and oiled me up, then his fingers. He put his mouth back on my clit and slowly worked one finger inside me. I clenched. "Do you want me to stop, Abbie? You only need to use your safe word."

"No, no. It's been a long time."

"Okay then, breathe. I'll go slow." I nodded at him. He worked his finger to the same rhythm he was using on my clit. I did a little deep breathing and then gave myself over to the sensations. It felt amazing. A hell of a lot better than with my ex, who had never even tried to prep me. We were young, and it had been spur of the moment. Someone taking care of you though, made all the difference.

He worked my clit with his tongue and, as I was getting close, worked a second finger inside. I grabbed his hair tighter as his other hand grasped my hip.

"Anderson, fuck! I am so close. Please keep doing that!" I begged. His mouth moved faster until he bit gently, and I came with a jerk. His fingers kept pumping my ass, a third added as I came down from my orgasm.

"I promise you, this is just your first orgasm. I will make this good for you, too," he said, standing.

"You already have," I cupped his cheek and flicked my tongue along his lips. He groaned.

"Little flower, just you wait." He stepped back, undid his pants, and slipped them off.

"Finally!" I said, reaching for his cock. I gave it a couple of strokes before he stilled my hand.

"Behave," he said. "On the bed with you."

I did as he said, waiting. "Well?" I demanded.

"Just enjoying the view." His weight shifted the bed. I twisted my head and spotted the oil and something that looked like a flower.

"That looks familiar," I remarked.

"It should. You have one." He handed it to me. "I want you to use it to make yourself come while I fuck this glorious ass of yours. Yes?"

"Yes," I said. I was so turned on right now.

He oiled his cock and reapplied oil to my ass. "Are you sure, Abigail?"

"Yes, Anderson."

"Are you ready, then?"

"Yes, Anderson."

He groaned. "It's so fucking hot when you say it that way." He slowly worked his cock into the tight opening, reapplying oil as necessary. Soon, I flicked on the toy he'd given me. Thanks to how he held me, I was able to balance myself while sending a prayer of thanks for years of yoga and Pilates. I had a strong core, and excellent balance. "That's it, baby. Make yourself come. You feel so fucking good right now. Are you doing alright?"

"I am," I said. "It feels good, actually." And it did. Much better than I expected.

"I am glad, little flower." He worked to keep pace with me as I got closer to my orgasm, and eventually, I came, clenching around his cock. "Fuck, Abigail! God, that feels amazing."

"You can move faster if you want," I told him. He did move faster, but he was still being careful. "Anderson, that feels so fucking good. You feel so good." He groaned my name, pulling me closer, kneading my breasts, and pinching my nipples. I dug my fingers into his thighs.

"I am so close, baby. Let me pull out."

"No," I said. "Come inside me. I want you to."

"Fuck, little flower! Thank you." He kept pumping faster as his teeth grazed my shoulder.

"Please," I whispered. "Oh, please."

He licked the spot where his teeth had been, then bit down, marking me as his orgasm started. I twisted to kiss him, and he came while our mouths fused in a savage kiss.

"Holy shit, Abbie." He was breathing heavily, and I nipped his jaw. "Thank you."

"Anytime. And I do mean that."

As his breathing returned to normal, he eased out of me slowly and brought me into the bathroom to take care of me. He was so gentle. "And you are sure you're fine?"

"I am fine. More than fine. I enjoyed that."

"Good, I'm glad." He carried me back into the bedroom, settled me in his bed, and climbed beside me. I rolled into him and promptly fell asleep.

ANDERSON

I watched Abbie sleep for a while. She had curled onto her side, one arm under her head, and her hair looked like it was growing wild from the pillow. She made soft snoring noises.

I looked at the time, quietly got out of bed, and went into the small office next to my bedroom. My father owned a cell phone but didn't like to use them and he didn't like it when we used them to call him. So, when I could, I called using a landline. "*Sojunghan adeul!*" he said jovially when he heard my voice. *Treasured son.* And even when I was mortal, that is how he had treated me—like a treasured son.

"*Abeoji*," I replied. "Are you well?"

"I am. It's lovely to hear your voice. How is everything going there?"

"Things are going well. Much of what Phillip did has been reversed." I paused, taking a deep breath. "I was calling to tell you something. To give you some good news. At least, I believe it's good news." My father's sadness was always that I chose to be alone. He had wanted me—all his children really—to find the same love he had found with my *eomeoni*. But I was the oldest now, and I know it pained him for me to be alone. He made me swear to tell him when I found someone.

And while I found it overly sentimental, and I was uncomfortable doing it, I loved and respected him. So, here we were.

"Ah, good! Enlighten me, please."

"I've found someone, *abeoji*." I winced a little. This was not in my comfort zone.

There was a moment of silence, then the fiercest vampire I have ever known laughed with joy. "You're in love? *igeos-i sasil-ibnikka?*"

"Yes, it's true," I answered.

"Tell me about her!" came the demand.

I spent several minutes telling him about Abbie while listening to ensure she was still asleep. "And I am hoping we can wrap up this issue this week. I don't like the thought of her being in any danger."

"Hmm, I think that's smart. You need to wipe these men from the face of the Earth. But discuss her uncle with her because I am not sure he should be allowed to live."

"I agree. She wants him to suffer. If he loses everything, including his freedom, that would satisfy her."

"This kind of person would go to a prison for the wealthy, though."

"Not this man. He will not be in a white-collar prison; I will see to that."

"I respect her decision, even if I do not agree with it. He can always have an accident at some point." He laughed, but it held no humor. "What of the woman?"

"I am not comfortable hurting a woman unless she presents an immediate threat to Abbie. I was going to hand her over to June. I believe that would be fitting punishment."

"Your sister? That may be worse than death." He was silent for a moment. "I approve."

"Thank you," I replied. Abbie's breathing changed. "Abbie is awake now, so I will phone tomorrow if that suits you."

"It does, yes. I am happy for you, son. I look forward to meeting her." With that, he hung up.

I padded back into the bedroom, and Abbie was winding her hair into a bun on top of her head. Christ, she was beautiful. "I thought I heard you speaking in Korean," she said. "Your father?"

"Yes," I said, crawling back into bed. Abbie immediately rolled over to cuddle into my side. "I hope I didn't wake you." I am not going to lie and say my life before her was lonely because it wasn't, no matter what my father chose to believe. And it wasn't empty. Hers hadn't been either, but it was better with her in it, and I knew she felt the same way. I can admit to a peace I have not felt for centuries, along with a fierce protectiveness. My father believed in fated loves, and while I am not sure I would admit to that, it did feel like we were meant to find each other.

"You didn't. I was somewhere between a light doze and full-on REM." She traced the tattoos on my chest. "Did you tell him about us?"

"I did. He is looking forward to meeting you."

"Is he? I didn't think he'd be interested in a lowly human."

"Oh, the love of his life was human. He doesn't think there is anything lowly about you all."

"I should stop jumping to conclusions."

"It's fine. Many vampires feel that way. Some of my family does, but not him. Despite what it may look like, I've never felt contempt for warmbloods."

"Hmm, I have a vampire question for you," she said.

"Go on," I replied. "You can ask me anything."

"It's a bit delicate, but okay. You all need blood to survive, yes?" I nodded. "What do *you* do for it? Is that too personal?"

"For someone else, yes. For you, no. I don't need to take in much blood at this point. I do mostly bagged blood. I take blood from humans, but generally when ..." I stopped.

She nodded. "When you need to kill them," she finished for me.

"Yes." I looked at her. "Is that an issue?"

"No. Maybe it should be. Maybe if you had to kill a beautiful woman or something and you drank her blood. You're good about eating the food I've cooked for you, though I know you are ambivalent about actual food. So, I've been wondering about the blood."

"I may be ambivalent about food for the most part, but I've found that I enjoy dining with you." In truth, taking meals with her filled me with contentment and joy. "You needn't worry about me taking the blood of any beautiful woman. I don't kill women if I can help it."

"So, you won't kill Miranda Summers?"

I shook my head. "Not outright. I am going to send her to my sister June. And I will be honest, Summers may not survive her."

"What will your sister do to her?"

"June is good with recalcitrant people. I am not totally sure what she does. She will find some job for her, and if Miranda toes the line, she'll survive. If she tries anything, June will kill her." I rubbed Abbie's back. "It's a bit of a cop-out—to send her away and not handle her myself—but again, I am squeamish about that."

"I understand," she said. "I do."

"That said, should she touch you, I will tear her apart."

"That shouldn't be hot, but it is."

"I am happy to keep saying it if it pleases you," I replied, smiling. "You're so bloodthirsty."

"I guess I am. What about my uncle?"

"I want to respect your wishes to not kill him. If he goes to a dangerous prison for life, that will have to do. He will suffer because he will lose everything." I pushed Abbie onto her back and hovered over her. "But, little flower, he will also die if he touches you."

"Yes, Anderson."

I growled a little at her. "Jennings and Deveraux are dead men. We'll speak to your father, and this will end, one way or another, within the week."

"Yes, Anderson."

"You know what it does to me when you say that in that particular voice, don't you?" I rolled a nipple between my fingers while she arched.

She looked at me, smiling. "Yes, Anderson."

I gave her a savage kiss. Her arms came around me, and she wrapped one leg around me.

"Mine," I said.

"Yours," she affirmed.

Words were unnecessary for quite some time.

***

I must have nodded off as I found Abbie in the kitchen the next morning, making breakfast in my button-down shirt—a large one by the look of it. I think I liked her in this look even more than the dress she had on last night. "Good morning," I said.

She looked up. "Morning!" She bounded over, kissed me, and moved back to the stove. "We never did have dinner, so I was starving this morning. I was pleasantly surprised to find food in the fridge. After what you said last night, I expected only bagged blood."

"I brought in groceries for you."

"Did you?" This delighted her.

"I did."

"Do you want some tea or um ... blood?"

The look on her face at this was comical, and I appreciated the effort. "No," I laughed. "I do not need any blood. I will make myself tea. What are we having for breakfast?"

I made my tea. I was as picky about it as Abigail was over her coffee. She watched me closely, though. She mentally noted the kind of tea I used and how I made it. "We're having pancakes, bacon, and fruit. You remembered syrup which is lovely."

"Sounds good," I said, and meant it. I hadn't lied to Abbie. I hadn't really cared about eating in the past, but I was becoming a domesticated villain, and I did not mind. Maybe Abbie was right about me.

"Good!" Her phone pinged. "Ah, shit."

"What's wrong?" And did I need to kill it?

"I forgot I scheduled lunch with the ladies today; Lacey, Cam, and Bree. Lacey wants to know where we're going."

"Why don't you have lunch downstairs? You can even have my booth. After lunch, we can go back to your place, maybe go over the gameplan with your dad tomorrow."

"Oh, I thought you would say we'd have more amazing sex."

"That's a given, Abigail."

"Perfect!" She laughed. "I will let the ladies know." She typed a message and got an almost immediate reply. "Oh, God, Lacey!" She looked at me. "She wants to meet you."

"Shouldn't be a problem." I'd do almost anything for her, so meeting her friends should be easy enough.

"You don't have to. But man, Bree would shit."

"What are they like?"

"Lacey is gregarious. She will literally tell you about her life within minutes if she likes you and her sex life soon after that. Cam is quieter—steady, but the kindest of us. She lives further downtown and is a teacher. Bree is a spoiled princess and a real bitch." I stared at her. "It's true. I am not sure why she still hangs out with us. Or why we let her." She flipped a couple of pancakes. "That's not totally fair. She can be generous and fun when she wants to be. She rarely wants to be anymore."

"You don't like her."

"No, I don't. Not really. She and Lacey had a thing in college. A thing which Bree won't even acknowledge anymore, and that infuriates me. I don't get why Lacey has a soft spot for her. Bree has always hated how close Lacey and I are, but we've been friends since we were kids."

Abbie pulled the bacon out of the oven and served breakfast. I took a bite. "Abigail, these pancakes are amazing! What's in them?"

"That's a secret. I cannot tell you."

"I'll force it out of you at some point. I only need to give you orgasms, and you are putty in my hands."

"Perhaps. But you will never get my mom's pancake recipe from me."

"We shall see, little flower, we shall see."

ABIGAIL

Lacey and Cam were excited about lunch at Anderson's restaurant. Bree was put out that she had to come downtown. But she was out-voted. Lacey got there first and careened into me, pulling me into her arms. "Oh, my God, you look so relaxed. Your skin is glowing! He must be fantastic in bed!"

"Lacey, for fuck's sake!" But I laughed. "Calm down. Have a seat!"

"What did I miss?" Cam said as she walked up.

"Nothing!" I replied, pulling her into a hug. Cam taught first grade and had the perfect temperament for it.

"My goodness, it is dark in here!" Bree's voice boomed. Anderson was by the bar, stone-faced. She pulled off her coat, tossed it to him, and walked back to us. I mouthed sorry, and he shook his head, handing her coat off to someone else.

"Bree, you just threw your coat at the owner," I said.

"Abigail, I highly doubt that. What would a vampire be doing hanging around the bar?" She whipped off her sunglasses and rolled her eyes at me. She then proceeded to give Cam and me a critical once-over. Cam reddened, and I tried not to punch her.

"Abbie would know if that was the owner," Lacey said as we sat. Cam was between Lacey and Bree, and Bree gave Cam a sour look. Cam winked at me. She was sweet, but she could get a little salty sometimes. She knew it irritated Bree when she wasn't next to Lacey.

"And how would Abigail know that?"

"Because Abbie is fucking the owner."

Cam's eyes widened. "Abbie! The owner is Anderson Jeon," —she looked around— "the vampire!" she said in a stage whisper. I caught Anderson trying not to laugh. Of course, he could hear her.

"Abigail, really now! You are not having relations with the owner!" Who the fuck even says 'relations' anymore? Fucking hell. "He's a vampire. Surely, you're smarter than that," Bree sniffed at me. I made a face. That woman has such a stick up her ass. She was nowhere near this bad in college. It's like her soul shriveled up and died.

"She's really not," Lacey quipped. I elbowed her, and she laughed.

I started to tell Bree off when Anderson slid up to the table. He was holding a champagne bucket with an icy bottle sitting in it. There was a server with him carrying a tray of champagne flutes who set the flutes on the table and faded into the background.

"Little flower," he said, his voice honey. "I brought you and your friends champagne." He set the bucket down, picked up my hand, and kissed my knuckles. Cam sighed, and Lacey muttered, "Damn!" under her breath. Bree's eyes widened, and she looked both horrified and angry.

"Thank you," I said, a little more breathlessly than I would have liked. "Anderson, this is Lacey, Cam, and Bree." I pointed to each lady in turn.

"Oh, I am so glad to meet you!" Lacey bounced in her seat.

"It's lovely to meet all of ... you." He gave Bree a hard look. *Fuck, I loved this guy.*

"It's nice to meet you," Cam said. "Abbie has a glow. We have you to thank for that. She deserves happiness." I blinked back tears. Cam had always been able to make me cry with the simplest and sweetest of sentiments.

Anderson smiled at her. "I agree, she does."

Bree sniffed. "This place is ... interesting," was all she said.

"Oh, I love it!" Cam said. "It's like a speakeasy!"

"Oh, you're right!" Lacey said.

"Abbie said much the same," Anderson replied. "I'm glad you like it. So, I had the chef prepare something special for all of you for lunch if you're amenable."

"Oh, that sounds great!" Lacey said.

"And lunch is my treat," he said.

"Hardly necessary," Bree said.

Anderson gave her another look. He was annoyed. "My lady and her friends do not pay for meals in my establishment."

"Thank you," Cam said emphatically. "When someone does something nice, Bree, we say thank you."

"I'm not one of your students, Cam."

"Then act like it, Breanna," came the reply. This sass from Cam was a delight. I hoped she was going to make a habit of it.

"Wonderful," Anderson replied. "I'll go speak with the chef, then." He gave me a soft but thorough kiss. "I will see you after lunch, little flower."

"Yes, Anderson." His eyes glittered as he gave me a wicked smile. I was very much aware of what he had done. He had let everyone in this restaurant know we were together. You messed with me at your own risk now. This news would travel back uptown, likely to those who put my father in prison. The kiss meant everything. Jacob Eastman's daughter had just been publicly linked to Anderson Jeon, vampire.

Lacey's expression was serious. "You're in love." Her voice was filled with wonder.

"Don't be ridiculous!"

"Bree, come on! Abbie is in love!" Lacey hugged me, laughing.

"More than that," Cam added. "He's in love with her."

They all stared at me. "It's true," I said. "I do love him, and he does love me." I looked at Bree. "And you can shut up about it. I don't give a flying fuck what you think."

Bree glared but said nothing. Cam changed the topic, and we talked about other things as we got course after course of the most amazing food.

"This has been amazing!" Cam said. "All of it." She dug into her dessert, a chocolate and whipped cream confection.

"You might want to be careful," Bree told her. "You don't need the extra weight." Cam turned red and looked down at her lap. Cam's weight was a sensitive topic. She and I both ran curvy, but Cam had struggled with her body image for years. Both her mother and father said awful things to her about it. When they bothered to talk to her at all, she had told us. She had worked hard on feeling good about herself and was thriving. So, to hit at Cam because she was mad at me was a step too far. It was cruel, and I wasn't having it.

I was about to tell her off when Cam glared at her. "Fuck off, Bree! I'm sorry you're such a miserable bitch, but you don't get to take it out on me. I'm sorry you're so jealous of Lacey and Abbie's friendship that you can't breathe." She looked at Lacey. "You have a soft spot for her, probably because parts of you have been inside her, but we're over it. She's shitty to me, she's shitty to your childhood friend, and enough is fucking enough."

I stared in shock. "Who are you?"

"I've had it with her!"

Bree's face was purple. I wanted to take a photo but restrained myself. Lacey shrugged at me, though her expression was sad. "Cam's right. I've spent years sticking up for you, and frankly, I am not even sure why. Maybe it's because I knew the sweeter side of you ..."

"Quite literally ..." I snickered.

"Not helping," she told me. "But Cam is right. I've let this go on too long. It stops now. You need to change your behavior and you need to get some help. Because Cam is right, you are miserable. I'm sorry that you're unhappy, but it's not Cam's or Abbie's fault."

"I don't need to sit here and listen to this!" Bree glared.

"No," I said. "You don't. You can go at any time."

Bree jumped up from the table. "You think you're better than me. But you aren't. Your father is a convicted criminal! A thief!"

I stood, fists balled by my side. Out of the corner of my eye I could see Anderson and Jack quickly making their way over. "I am a better person than you because I am not a bitter, roaring bitch. Yes, my dad is in prison, but that has nothing to do with why you are such a misery to be around. Bringing him up is cruel. And you've always been a bitch, but cruelty is new for you."

"And come on, Bree, we all know Abbie's dad didn't do it." I smiled at Cam. I hadn't realized she didn't think he was guilty. I knew Lacey didn't.

"Do we, though?"

"Bree, I am about to knock you on your ass!" I went for her, and Anderson pulled me back. "Anderson! Did you hear her? Let me go!"

"I did, baby. You can beat the fuck out of her if you want. I'd prefer you do it outside."

"Oh, well. That's reasonable. You can let go." He did. "Let's go, sunshine. You and me, outside!"

Bree walked over to me. "Your father is dirty, and so are you. I told Lacey she should dump you and let you rot here."

Lacey groaned, and Anderson sighed, "Go ahead, Abbie." I made a fist, pulled back, and broke her nose.

"My nose!" She howled.

"Oh, relax!" I said. "It's not even the one you were born with."

"Mrs. Larson," Anderson must have had Jack do a little research on my friends. "It's time you left. You're not welcome back. And neither is your philandering husband."

Oh, shit! We all knew it, and so did she. But no one had ever said it out loud. Anderson really was the eyes and ears of this city.

"I am going to call the cops!" She held a napkin to her nose.

"I wouldn't do that," Anderson said silkily. "It won't go well for you."

"And I have pictures from college of you and Lacey. I will put them out on social media," I said, giving her a haughty look. "Lacey is no one's dirty little secret, and how dare you ever treat her as such." One day, Lacey and I would need to discuss why she had ever let this woman do that. But not today.

She paled and then stormed out. "I hope she remembers her coat," Anderson said, "because it will be trash by the night's end." He pulled me to him. "You are a tigress, aren't you?" He sounded ridiculously pleased by this.

"Oh, if you wanted someone dealt with in college, you got Abbie to handle it," Cam said. I looked over at her, but she was staring at Jack. And Jack was staring back.

"Really now? Anderson asked.

Lacey nodded, though she was watching Jack and Cam as well. "We'd harness all that rage of hers and point her at the offender."

I shrugged. "I rarely had to hit someone. But I would if I needed to."

"You surprise me more every day, little flower."

I leaned against him and sighed contentedly. Lacey's phone pinged. "Ah, that's Peter. We're off to his parents for the next week. Meh. But it's at the beach, and the beach makes me horny."

"Life makes you horny," I snorted.

"True. Oh, that means I can't take Cam home." Lacey's voice was all innocence.

"Oh," Jack cleared his throat. "I would be happy to take your friend home." He looked at Anderson. "If that is alright with you."

"If it's fine with Miss Hoskins, it's fine with me."

"Miss Hoskins? May I see you home?"

Cam blinked. "Only if you call me Cam," she said. "You are?"

"I'm Jack. Shall we go, Cam?"

She nodded, peeled her eyes off him for a moment to hug Lacey and me, thank Anderson for lunch, and was gone.

I turned to Lacey. "Now, you know you pass her apartment to get on the highway to the beach."

Lacey grinned. "I know! But I have never seen her look that way at someone. And he returned it. So, I helped."

"Jack has *never* looked at anyone that way, at least as long as I've known him."

"Peter is outside, so I do need to go." She hugged me and looked at Anderson. "I am trusting you with my best girl. I don't care if you're a big tough vampire. If you hurt her, I will stake you myself."

"Lacey!" I was shocked.

Anderson threw back his head and laughed. "Lacey, I promise to take good care of her."

"You'll help get her dad out?"

"I promise you, Lacey. We'll get her dad out of prison."

"Are you going to kill people?"

"Fuck, Lacey!" My bestie was sometimes a lot.

"Yes, Lacey. I am."

Lacey looked at him for a second, then nodded. She kissed him on the cheek. His shocked expression made me laugh. "Good enough!" Then, she was out the door.

"So," I said, turning to him. "Those are my friends."

"I like them. Well, not Bree. But I don't think we need to worry about her anymore."

"I don't think we do. So, everyone in here knows we're together now."

"They do. They know you *and* your friends are under my protection."

I nodded. "You're okay with that?"

"More than okay, little flower."

"So, Jack?" I asked.

"In the years he's worked for me, several female and male vampires have tried to turn his head. He was polite, but he had no interest."

"I've never seen Cam stare at someone that long." I bit my lip. "He'll be ... he won't ..."

"If I thought there was any reason to worry, I would not have let him drive her home. He will take care with her."

I nodded. "Thank you," I rested my head against his chest, and he put his arms around me. I heard the murmurs but ignored them. They didn't matter.

"Lunch was more than you bargained for. We'll go back to your place and talk through tomorrow. I need to come back here this evening though."

I nodded. "Okay. Can you come back after you close?"

"Nothing on Earth will stop me, Abigail."

"You didn't hear that," I said.

"Hear what?" Jack asked.

"Remind me to raise your salary," I replied.

"I must admit, since Abigail, you keep wanting to pay me more. I approve."

"So, your initial trepidation is gone?"

Jack shook his head. "It is. She is perfect for you, and you for her."

I nodded. "She is perfect for me." I cleared my throat. "Once again, this conversation never happened."

"What conversation?"

The car stopped.

"We're here."

***

We walked into the warehouse, and Deveraux was already there, tied to a chair and gagged. He looked both furious and petrified. Good. That would make this more fun.

"Gun," I snapped. It was in my hand immediately. I walked to Deveraux and looked down at him, saying nothing. I sighed, hitting him across the face with the gun. He tried to scream around the gag.

"Shut up!" Deveraux stopped, but began to whimper quietly. "Take off his gag, please."

"Is this your gun?" My voice was calm. Too calm. Everyone else cringed to hear it. I was beyond furious. He didn't answer. "I am asking you a question, Deveraux. Is this your gun?" I slammed it into his face again.

He whimpered, nodding at me. His eyes held wildfire. I hoped he'd try to make a deal with me. Oh, I did so love when they thought they could escape me. It made the end that much sweeter.

"Speak!"

"Yes," he spat out. "It's my gun!"

"And were you planning on using this gun on Abigail?"

"Yes. The bitch has it coming. She's ruining everything!" I hit him again.

"Were you told by Jennings or Woodman to do this?" He shook his head. "You decided to take care of this yourself?" He nodded. He probably wanted to prove himself to Jennings and Woodman. He wanted to show them that he was as capable as they were, but deep down, he knew he was expendable.

I sighed. "I am astonished you thought it would work. You are colossally stupid. Did you not think I would protect my woman? Or were you counting on me being like my brother?"

"Your woman? Abbie is a nice piece of ass, but ..." I took my foot and tipped his chair over so he was on his side. He howled in pain as he hit the floor.

"I would tell you not to speak like that about her ever again, but your time is short. Still, let's not push our luck, shall we?"

Deveraux whimpered. "Fucking asshole!"

I shrugged. "What you call me doesn't matter." I got onto my haunches, putting the gun barrel to his head. "What you call her does matter. Be mindful of that. You are going to die, but I'd like to have a conversation before we have some fun." I laughed, but there was no mirth in it. "Well, before I have some fun. Are you going to behave and answer my questions? Or do we end it here?" I dug the gun harder into his head.

"I'll talk ..." he almost sobbed. Fuck, this man was pathetic.

"Lift him, please." I gestured to the vampires next to the chair. Death was staring Deveraux in the face. Did he think he could save himself? Death would not be cheated, though. Not today.

"I've been listening to your conversations. You, Jennings, and Summers. But none with Woodman. I find that interesting. We've hacked all your phones and emails. So, tell me how you're doing it?"

"Burner phones," Deveraux rasped. "Woodman insisted. We use them out in public spaces. Woodman, Jennings, and I also leave messages for each other at the gym."

I had not thought they'd be bright enough for burner phones. That's on me. "Where is your burner phone?"

"In my car. Back at Abigail's ..."

"You are not to say her name again." I looked at Jack.

"On it," he replied, typing into his phone.

"How often do you change the phones out?"

"Once every couple of weeks." Deveraux coughed and spat out a few teeth. And right after having them fixed. Such a shame.

"And this was Woodman's scheme?" He nodded. "Why?" No answer. "I asked you why?"

"I don't know. I've never known!"

"Then why do this? What is in it for you exactly? If you say money, I may need to kill you quickly. That would be so boring."

"Because Ab—Miss Eastman was a stuck-up bitch who thought she was better than me."

"She is better than you. And that was the problem. She found out how bad you were at your job, didn't she? She quietly fixed your mistakes, never saying anything to anyone. But she mentioned them to you in passing, didn't she? You got nervous. You thought she'd tell the CEO, which just proves you didn't really know her at all." Abigail had put up with Deveraux for years. If she was going to report him, she'd have done it long ago.

"She wanted my job!"

I shook my head. I didn't believe that for a minute. "No, she didn't. You thought she did. And you didn't like she had something on you and that she wouldn't sleep with you." I thought about breaking his kneecaps, but I decided against it. "So, when Jennings came to you with this, you jumped at the chance. Jacob and Abigail Eastman not only excel at their jobs but are respected and well-liked. Jacob knew Jennings was embezzling, so he had to do something to shift the blame away. Woodman presented the perfect opportunity for this. Jennings grabbed it, and dragged you along, is that it?." I shrugged, not really caring if I had it right. "Maybe you were dipping your fingers in, too, and you thought you'd be discovered."

"How dare you!"

"It doesn't matter," I continued, ignoring him. "You're the weak link. You react with emotion. You don't think things through. Like today. And that means you die sooner."

He thrashed in his seat. "Wait! I can help you! I know things."

"You don't," I replied. "And that's rather the problem. Untie and lift him!" I gestured to the two vampires behind him.

I handed the gun to Jack and went to stand in front of Deveraux. "Here is what will happen: I will be sporting and give you a head start. The doors and windows are all locked and guarded, so you can't escape that way. I will count to three, and then I want you to run. If you can outrun or outsmart me, you may live." He wouldn't do either. But if, by some miracle, he did best me, he would still die. You can count liar among my many sins.

"You're going to hunt me?"

"Oh, I see that feeble brain of yours is keeping up. Yes, I am going to hunt you. And when I catch you, I am going to drain you dry. I will enjoy watching the light leaving your eyes. Then, I am going to go to the woman you could never have."

I had the pleasure of his face paling and his eyes turning wild and frightened. "You ... you ..."

"One ... two ...." I paused, "Three! Run!" Surprisingly, he took off like a shot. The survival instinct was strong. It wouldn't last.

Jack cackled. "I didn't think he'd actually run."

"Me neither." I waited a few minutes. "This shouldn't take long." I could hear him climbing the first set of stairs.

I took my shoes off and started after him. I didn't hurry. There was no need to. I'd be able to catch him easily. He was panting and making all sorts of noises. I could smell the fear coming off him in waves.

"Oh, Mason," I called out. "You can run, but you can't hide. Not from me." I laughed as he started to cry. "You're getting much further than I thought you would. Look at you go. You'd almost think you were going to make it."

"You fucking monster!" he yelled.

I tsked. "So brave now that the end is near." I stopped and let him wander a bit. Once he got to the third floor, it was all over.

I climbed the stairs to the second floor. "I am coming for you, Mason."

He stopped, trying to catch his breath, then hit the stairs to the third floor. I followed him.

"Mason, Mason, Mason," I sing songed. "It's fruitless, you know. I am going to end your life. And you'll die like the sniveling coward you are. Rest assured, I will make it hurt."

Ah, there it was. He pissed himself. Yet, he kept going until he hit the bricks. Literally. There were several booby traps designed to stop someone. He didn't even get past the first one: a pile of bricks. I reached him in no time. He was lying across the bricks, his left foot at an odd angle.

"Looks like you broke your foot, Mason." I picked him up by the collar. "Well, never mind. It won't hurt for long." I pushed him against the wall. "But it will hurt dreadfully." I broke one arm, then the other. His two legs followed.

"Please ... please ..." The fact he could still speak would have impressed me if I cared.

"Please, what?"

"Don't kill me. Let me live." His voice was barely a whisper. He was in such pain. But he didn't know true pain yet.

I looked him dead in the eyes and went, "No." My fangs descended, and I ripped open his neck. He screamed but could do nothing, thanks to his broken limbs. I drained him of every drop of blood and made sure the pain he felt as I did, was hell on Earth.

Before he died, I pulled back briefly. "Know this: no one will care you're dead. No one will remember you. No one will mourn you." And with that, I drained the last of his blood.

I pulled back and dropped him where he was. Then, I walked away.

When I got downstairs, Jack held out a towel and a bottle of water. "Thank you," I said. I wiped the blood from my face, neck, and hands. Then, I rinsed my mouth.

"I'll have the body disposed of," Jack said.

"Thank you again." I looked up. "This doesn't bother you?"

"You've never asked me that before. But no, it doesn't." He cracked a small smile. "I'd be shit at my job if it did."

"True," I said. I took a deep breath. I'd be lying if I said I didn't enjoy that. The fresh blood would keep me going for a long time. My body was humming, though, like a live wire. It was the adrenaline coursing through me. I did my best to calm down and even out my breathing. I needed to get to Abbie. I needed to see her, hold her. I knew she was safe, but I wouldn't feel right again until I was with her.

"Let's get you to Abigail," Jack said as if reading my thoughts. "We don't have another shirt for you. But I think it will be fine. She doesn't seem squeamish."

"Thank you Jack," I replied. "Getting to Abbie is exactly what I need to do right now." I just hoped seeing me like this wouldn't make her turn away.

ABIGAIL

I was pacing back and forth in my living room, waiting for Anderson. Logically, I knew he would be fine and come out on top. But it was still hard not to worry.

"Miss," Keith said. "He'll be alright, you know that, right?"

"She does," Soames replied. "But knowing it and feeling it are not the same thing. Especially when love is involved." I looked at her in surprise. She shrugged. "It doesn't take a genius to see how you two feel about each other."

I gave her a small smile. "No, I guess it doesn't." I sighed. "Okay, I am going to make coffee. Do you two want any?" They shook their heads, but as I made my way into the kitchen, there was a loud knock at the door.

"Who is it?" Soames called out.

"It's Anderson!"

"Prove it!" She looked at me. "His instructions," was all she said.

"The first thing you said to me when I found you was, 'Please make sure my son is safe. If you do, I'll follow you anywhere.'" Soames had been a mother, it seems. Somehow that made sense, and I felt such compassion for her. I wouldn't let it show, I didn't think she'd appreciate that.

Soames blinked a few times, an intense sadness settling in her eyes, and opened the door. "Sir," she said.

"Well done," he said to her as he nodded at Keith. "But now, out!" The two hustled out quickly.

I saw blood on his shirt and neck, but he looked whole. His eyes were dark, ringed with amber, and the look he gave me was of such love and need that it took my breath away.

I opened my arms, and he was instantly across the room to me. I wound them around his neck, and he picked me up. I wrapped my legs around his waist as he stalked to my bedroom. He sat on the bed and buried his nose in my neck, inhaling deeply. He shuddered, inhaled again, and groaned softly.

"Fuck," he said. "I could happily drown in your scent." I stroked his hair as we sat there, almost feeling the adrenaline coursing through him.

"Shower?" I asked.

"If you take it with me," he said, lifting his head. He nipped my bottom lip and then kissed me hard. I gripped him tighter, and his hands dug into my ass. I groaned, and his tongue swept into my mouth. Mine met his, and they tangled as the kiss took on more urgency. He stood and carried me into the bathroom, not breaking the kiss until we backed into the sink.

"Little flower," he said, his voice hoarse.

"It's okay, baby. I've got you." However, I had to let him go to turn the shower on. I unbuttoned his shirt, slid it off his shoulders, and ran my hands along his chest. I unbuttoned his pants next. "You forgot to take off your shoes."

He smiled slightly. "Don't tell my father about this, hmm? Bad manners." He stepped out of them.

"Your secret is safe with me," I answered as I lowered his pants so he could step out of those. Once he was naked, I took his cock in my hand and stroked him.

"God, fuck, Abbie!"

I gestured for him to get into the shower. I stripped quickly and got in with him. I grabbed a washcloth and the shower gel and soaped him up, starting at his neck.

"You missed some blood here," I said.

"Oh, you don't have to …"

"I don't mind. Hush now." I washed his body as he watched me with those eyes of his. "Don't get used to this," I said. "Just sometimes."

"I promise to return the favor," he said.

Once he was clean, I dropped to my knees, taking his cock in my mouth. He hissed out a breath. "Abbie," he said, groaning. He grabbed my hair and tugged me gently as I took more of him in my mouth. I gagged at first but soon adjusted. I licked, sucked, and even gave him a gentle nip. I was gratified that while one hand was in my hair, the other was braced on the wall.

"I love how you look with my cock in your mouth, little flower. That's it, suck me harder now." I did as he told me. "*Chaghan yeoja*," he said silkily.

I pulled back. "Did you … what does that mean?"

"Good girl," he said. *Shit, that was hot.* I took him in my mouth and sucked him even harder than before. The noises he made spurred me on.

He pulled me off him after a few minutes. I looked at him in confusion before he lifted me. "I want to come in that pretty little pussy of yours, Abbie." He pushed me against the wall. "Are you wet, baby?" His fingers found my clit and rubbed. "Oh, you are wet, so very wet." He dropped to his knees and pushed my legs apart. He found his marks on my thighs and sucked each into his mouth while I grabbed his hair and moaned loudly.

"Anderson!"

"You like it when I mark you, don't you?" I nodded. "Use your words, Abigail."

"Yes, Anderson."

"Yes, Anderson, what?"

"Yes, Anderson, I like it when you mark me." He bit, and I bucked against his mouth.

"I like marking you." He bit the other side and stood, lifting me. I wrapped my legs around him. "But I love fucking you more." With that, he thrust his cock into me, and I screamed. "Hold onto me, baby." I latched onto his shoulders.

He bent and took a nipple into his mouth as he pumped mercilessly. He sucked the nipple as I arched to give him better access. "Harder," I panted.

He lifted his head and gave me a rough kiss as his thrusts got harder and rougher. "Such a good girl, but so dirty," he said, giving my ear a small nip. I bent my head and bit into his shoulder, and he groaned my name.

He fucked me harder, bracing me so I wouldn't smack into the shower wall, but I couldn't get enough of him. I bit. I scratched. I practically clawed at him. "Anderson, please!"

"Please, what, my dirty angel? Do you want to come?"

"Yes! I want to come! Please! Fuck!" He put his hand between us and massaged my clit. "God, yes, please!" I nearly sobbed as my orgasm came closer. He bore down on my clit, and I came, bucking against him. But he wouldn't let up as he chased his own orgasm.

"I think you have another one in you," he said. "I want you to come again, little flower. With me." His thrusts were savage at this point, as were his fingers on my clit. As he came closer, so did I. All at once, we both came, screaming.

He turned off the water, and we both stood there, twined together, soaking wet and trying to remember how to breathe normally. "Little flower," he said. "If I were mortal, this probably would have killed me. You are everything I have ever wanted. I am never letting you go."

"Maybe just to dry off?" I asked, kissing his nose.

He laughed. "Well, maybe for that, then. But just that."

***

Despite Anderson's best intentions to not let me go, he did have to go back to the restaurant to deal with some issues that had cropped up. I ended up not seeing him until he picked me up the next morning to visit my father.

He smiled at me. "I prefer you in one of my shirts, but these jeans run a close second."

"Not the corset dress?" I asked.

"Oh, don't get me wrong, I love that dress. But you are most yourself dressed as you are now."

"That's good to know, since I am in jeans most of the time." I stroked his cheek. "Thank you for doing the driving today," I said.

He smiled at me, squeezing my hand. "I don't drive a lot, but I know how to, and I thought you'd prefer it to be the two of us."

"You were correct," I sighed. "I am nervous, and I hate visiting him there. I hate seeing him in prison. It breaks my heart and infuriates me. I want to punch something."

"I understand. This will be the last time you need to visit him in prison. We'll finish it this week. It's already set in motion with Deveraux's death." I had made him tell me how it went down. I only flinched a few times. If you asked me if he deserved what he got, right now, I'd say yes. Maybe when this was over, I'd change my mind. But I doubted it.

He continued. "As for punching something, I have a punching bag. Have you ever used one?" I shook my head. "You will learn. I will teach you. You can take out some of that aggression without hitting someone."

"Will it help?"

"I think so, yes."

"I want to hit a person right now, though."

"Miranda Summers," he replied.

I brightened up a little. "Oh nice, good call." I looked out the window. "I have an idea about how to handle her."

He nodded. "Excellent. I will follow your lead. My sister will be here tomorrow to take her. Will that work?"

"It will. After we visit Dad, I will tell you what I'm thinking."

"Sounds good."

"Jennings?"

"I originally thought to handle him and Summers at the same time. But I am not sure that will fit into your plan."

"I can make it work," I replied."

"Are you certain? I can adjust my plan."

I smiled at him. "I appreciate that. But if we have them together and Jennings sees Miranda will live, he may get lulled into a false sense of security. Then you can rip it away from him."

"You are a bloodthirsty little flower, aren't you? I like it. You do not have to stay when I kill him."

"I want to, I think. Are you going to play with your food?"

He laughed. "No, I am going to kill him quickly. I will not think less of you if you change your mind or step out."

"I know you won't." Right now, I was feeling fine about it, but who knows how I'd feel in the moment.

"Then we will deal with your uncle. Together."

"Together," I affirmed.

"I will not kill your uncle unless I have to."

"If he touches me, you mean?"

"Yes, that is what I mean."

I paled a little but nodded. "Fair. But if not, he loses everything, goes through a messy trial, and spends the rest of his life in prison."

"Of course, Abigail." I narrowed my eyes at him. How long would Uncle Evan spend in prison before an accident befell him?

***

Anderson managed to secure a private room for us to visit Dad. I don't know how he did it, but I was grateful. The door opened, and a guard marched my dad in. He looked older than when I had seen him last month.

"Cuffs off, and leave the room," Anderson said to the guard.

"Oh," the guard said hesitantly. "I don't think I can ..."

"You can. Do it. Now." The guard looked around, and Anderson sighed. "There are no windows here, and you'll be standing outside. Do it." The young man did as he was told and scuttled out of the room.

I ran over, and my dad enveloped me in a big hug. "Sweetheart," he said. "It's so good to see you!"

"It's good to see you too, Dad." I pulled back and sniffled. He'd always been my rock and made me feel safe. Now Anderson was filling that void, and I was stupidly worried I would feel differently about him, but I didn't.

He smiled at me and looked at Anderson. "Anderson Jeon, it's about time you showed up."

"You were expecting him?"

"I was," he said, his arm around me. He looked at me, then him, and nodded to himself. "I see. Let's sit. We probably don't have long."

"We have," Anderson said, "as long as we need. It's a pleasure to meet you, Mr. Eastman." Anderson put out his hand, and my dad shook it.

Once we were seated, I looked at Dad. "Why were you expecting Anderson?"

"I was expecting someone from the Jeon family."

"I don't understand," I said to Anderson. "I thought you knew nothing about this?"

"I don't," Anderson said. "Mr. Eastman, your daughter, and I have been working to find the proof to free you. We know how this all started and are about to finish it."

"So, you do have the information I sent you?"

"Sir?" said Anderson while I said, "Daddy?"

"Sweet girl, I told you to find the files. But I was hoping they'd find you." He looked pointedly at Anderson. "But maybe you should explain how you got here first." When my dad used that tone, he wouldn't budge. Anderson nodded at him.

We explained everything but left the nature of our relationship purposely vague. As we told the story and Anderson explained Deveraux's part, I saw something I had never seen before on my dad's face—fury. "Dad, do you know why Uncle Evan is so pissed off that he would do this?"

"I should have known he was involved. It's all about money."

"It can't be just money," I said.

"It is. Several years ago—this was years after your mom had died—Evan came to me and told me his company was floundering. Of course it was, the man is a moron. He needed money. He asked, and I said no. More than that, I laughed in his face." Dad rubbed his hand over his face. "And then I told him exactly what I thought of him and that family. I had held my tongue for your mother, but she was gone, and I blew up at him. He said he wanted your mom's trust fund back; your trust fund now. I told him to go fuck himself. He said he'd sue me for it, but he had no legal leg to stand on, and he knew it. His intention was to make things messy for us. Then, I really blew up. I punched him."

"Dad!"

Anderson laughed. "Well, I see where your daughter gets her temper."

"It's true. You do get it from me."

"No, Dad. I've never seen you angry. Ever."

"Oh, sweetie, I got angry when you were very small, and it scared you. Badly. I swore I'd never show you that side of myself again. And I haven't. But you're an adult and should know your dad gets angry."

"So, you are angry you're in here?" I asked.

"Furious." He looked at Anderson. "Before I got arrested, I had a courier pick up electronic copies of all the files and deliver them to you. I suppose it was your brother I sent them to."

"May I ask why me, Mr. Eastman?"

"You can call me Jacob, and ... well, it was silly. But I've met you before—as a child."

Recognition dawned on Anderson's face. "Eastman! Eastman Electronics belonged to your family."

I smiled at the memory of the store. I loved that place when I was small. When they finally decided to close the store, I was sad to lose such a fun playground.

"It did, indeed. You helped us when we were being harassed by some local wise guys. You told me to let you know if I ever needed help. I sent a note to you with the files."

"Jacob, I am so profoundly sorry this has happened to you, and I failed to help."

"You're helping now."

"We could have avoided all of this." Anderson stood. "Will you excuse me for a moment?" We both nodded at him, and he left the room. A few moments later, I heard him shouting in Korean. I assumed at his brother.

"I like him," Dad said. "I like you two together."

"How did you know we were together?"

"I'm your father, sweetheart. I know when I've been replaced."

"Dad, no! No one can replace you."

"Yes, he can. As it should be." Dad tugged my hair. "But if he hurts you, he'll have me to answer to."

"He'll never hurt me." If I was sure of anything, it was that.

"He'd better not."

ANDERSON

I walked back into the room. "Thank you," I said. "I apologize. I spoke with my brother, then phoned Jack. We know where the package is, and it will await us when we return to town." I was furious at my brother, and so was our father. It brings shame to the family to ignore any sincere plea for help. I review all requests personally for this reason. "Once again, my family and I apologize for this."

"You didn't yell as much as I would have thought," Abbie said.

"My father started in on him, and while I am furious, I did not think it was quite fair to gang up on Phillip." In truth, my father had been calm, and that was chilling. Phillip was in serious trouble, and I felt a small amount of compassion for him. I have been on that end of Father's disappointment. It is not a good place to be.

Jacob nodded. "So, next steps?"

Abbie outlined her plan for Miranda Summers, and I weighed in on Jennings and Woodman. "Jacob, would you be willing to take the CFO position for Allied Tech?" I asked.

Jacob thought for a moment. "Temporarily, while someone else is found. I'd like to retire. But I will help you find a replacement."

I nodded. "Fair. Your retirement benefits and pension will be reinstated." He'd retire as the CFO, and his compensation package would reflect that.

"What about my company?" Abbie asked.

"Abigail, as of tomorrow, you're acting CFO." Her eyes widened. She hadn't even thought of it.

"I don't want it!"

"I know, love. I need you to stay until a replacement is found. Like with your father. Can you do that?"

She thought for a few minutes, then nodded. "I can. Hopefully, it won't take long."

"I don't think it will. I have a couple of ideas." I looked at her. "What do you want to do then? I think I know, but I am curious if I am correct."

"I want to start my own firm and help smaller businesses get ahead. I've been doing a bit of that lately and realized how much I've missed it."

"That's how I started," Jacob said. "Since you specialized in tax law, you can probably put that degree to use. Finally." He smiled at me.

"Ah, I'd forgotten you had a law degree," I said. "So smart!"

"I'm very proud of you. And I would love to help. In a consulting way, not full-time."

"I'd love that, Dad!"

"Good. Now, I need to talk to Anderson." He gave her a pointed look. I knew what was coming. I didn't think he would warn me off his daughter, but he would have a heart-to-heart with me about her.

"Why?" Abbie asked.

"You know why, sweetie. Step outside and give us a few minutes. Please?"

"This is so old-fashioned of you," she said.

"I am an old-fashioned guy," her father replied. "Abigail, please." That tone again.

Abbie bit her lower lip but nodded and stepped out.

Jacob looked at me for a moment. "My daughter is in love with you."

"Yes, sir. And I am in love with her."

"I surmised as much. She's human. Are you really going to love her for the rest of her life? Because it's much shorter than yours." Jacob Eastman pulled no punches. I expected nothing less when it came to his only child.

"With everything I am." It was as simple as that. I would love that woman until whatever end was in store for us, then well beyond. Twelve hundred years is a long time to be alive. To be in love for the first time, I would make the most of it.

Jacob cleared his throat. "I can see you mean that, son." He laughed. "Sorry. You're older than I am, but looking at you, it's difficult to remember that. What if she wants to become a vampire?"

There it was. The unspoken thing that not even Abbie and I had discussed. But it was there. It was *always* there in human and vampire relationships. "That decision is a long way off. But it will be a decision for Abbie and myself. And only us."

Jacob smiled. "Understood." He paused a moment, choosing his words. "My daughter means the world to me. Everything I did was for her and her mother. I made some bad decisions. Taking that job at Allied Tech may have been one, but it seemed a good idea at the time."

"I have no doubt it was." In the end, Jacob was an outsider, and people weren't always kind to outsiders. Abbie's uncle could have done this no matter where Jacob Eastman had landed a job.

"It enabled me to do things for Abbie I may not have been able to otherwise." He ran his hands through his hair. "I have worried about her being an only child and not finding someone. I don't need to worry anymore about her being alone. But being with you also paints a target on her back."

"Yes," I replied. I would not lie to this man. "There is a certain danger to being with me. But there is also safety to it. No one can protect her as I can."

"Some would say she wouldn't need it if she weren't with you."

"I think this situation proves this is not necessarily the case. Your daughter was unaware of the danger she was in before I came to the scene. She was blithely plotting an overthrow without knowing Jennings wanted to kill her and Deveraux wanted ... that does not matter now."

"Why did you kill him?"

"Because of Abbie. He was an idiot. He could have survived this, but he made it known that he was a danger to her."

Jacob's face morphed, and I clearly saw the anger and disgust there. "Then I won't lie, I am glad he's dead. Did he die like the sniveling jackass he's always been?"

"He absolutely did."

"Good." His voice was hard, but he looked exhausted. Being here was taking a toll on him.

"We need to get you out of here," I said gently.

"It has not been a restful year."

"I don't understand why you were put in a medium and not minimum-security prison."

"My brother-in-law had pull there, I think."

"Ah," I replied. "Well, once you're out, I will take care of that."

"And I'll let you," Jacob smiled. "Okay, let's put Abbie out of her misery and get her back in here."

***

Abbie turned to me on the ride home. "What did you and my father talk about?"

I smiled at her. "He wanted to know if my intentions were pure."

"He did not!"

"Basically, yes. He did."

"Oh, my fucking God! What did you say?"

"That my thoughts were decidedly impure as they pertained to you."

"Anderson!" She sounded horrified.

I laughed. "Abbie, of course, I didn't say that. I told him that, yes, my intentions were pure. That I loved you and would always love and protect you."

"Oh." She blinked tears away. "Did he ask if you would make an honest woman out of me?"

"No, but he did ask if I was going to make you a vampire."

"That's none of his business. I love him, but he had no right to ask you that."

"No, but he's your father. He loves you and is concerned about you."

"I know, but we haven't even talked about that."

"No, and we don't need to right now. It is a conversation that can wait. This is still rather new for us."

"True. What if I don't want to become a vampire?"

"That changes nothing. I will love you for all your life, however long or short that may be. I will mourn you for the rest of my existence once you leave this Earth. But I would not miss loving you for all the world."

"Oh. Oh, Anderson," her voice was wobbly, "that is the most romantic thing anyone has ever said to me. Or, probably to anyone."

"I do not say it to be romantic, but I am glad you found it so. I say it because it is the truth."

"That's why it's romantic. Remind me to kiss you when we get out of this car."

"Why wait?" I pulled the car over to the side of the road and put it in park. Abbie undid her seatbelt and launched herself at me. She took my face in her hands and kissed me softly but thoroughly. I stroked her back as she mapped my mouth with her own. I let her lead the kiss, and she took her time.

It was the sweetest kiss I'd ever been gifted.

She pulled away after kissing the tip of my nose. "I love you with everything I am and everything I will ever be," she said.

"Also, very romantic." I smiled at her.

"Because it's true. But I was honestly trying to be a little romantic." She sat back in her seat. "Now, let's go put a plan in place."

"As you wish, my tigress."

ABIGAIL

Anderson, Jack, and I talked for several hours about our plan before they had to leave to attend to other business and let me get some rest. A rumor about Deveraux disappearing began to circulate late Sunday evening. This was swiftly followed by a phone call from the CEO, asking me to take on the interim CFO role. I humbly accepted the position.

I then set up a meeting with Miranda Summers in Deveraux's office for the next morning. I did not take no for an answer. Anderson's men would pick Jennings up and smuggle him inside the building.

"How exactly are you planning on that?" I asked him over a video chat.

"Don't concern yourself about that, little flower."

I stared at him. "Is he already there?"

"Oh, no, I want him full of righteous indignation about us grabbing him tomorrow. Full of bluster and bravado. It's more entertaining that way."

"For whom?"

"For me," he answered, baring his fangs at me.

I rolled my eyes at him. "You're terrible."

"I am rather terrible. I am a scary vampire, after all."

"I am terrified of you." I laughed.

"Are you mocking me? Maybe I need to show you how ferocious I can be, Abigail."

"I know you can be terrifying, but I am not scared of you."

"Abigail, I would sooner cut off a limb than harm you. You need never be scared of me." His tone was so serious. My heart melted a little.

"I know that, Anderson, I really do." I yawned.

"Are you sleepy finally?"

"I think so."

"Go rest, little flower. I will see you tomorrow."

"'Night, I love you."

"And I love you."

Honestly, this love thing was pretty great.

***

The next morning, I sat behind Deveraux's desk, waiting for Miranda. I wore an older designer suit that belonged to my mother with stiletto heels I liked to call, 'Come fuck me, shoes.' This was a situation where image was important. I was going to war and had to be dressed for battle.

Someone knocked, and Deveraux's secretary Kacey poked her head in. "Ms. Eastman? Miranda Summers is here for you." Kacey was her usual bubbly self. How shitty had it been to be his assistant if someone else sitting behind his desk didn't even faze you. While I was in this role, I'd make sure she got a pay raise. I have no doubt she deserved one.

"You can send her in. Thanks, Kacey."

The door opened wider, and Miranda stepped in. She looked like shit. She'd obviously gotten no sleep and looked haggard and worn out. She, too, was wearing a designer suit along with the signature single strand of pearls she always wore. I wanted to choke her with them. Her ash blonde hair was in a French twist, but there were loose strands, something unusual for her.

120

I let her stand for a moment while I typed onto Deveraux's computer. I finally looked up. "Miranda, hello. You can have a seat. I will be with you in a moment."

I continued to type. This was Anderson's idea. It was designed to make her even more fidgety and nervous than she already was. It would also piss her off that I was ignoring her. Her opinion of me was low, and my position of power and authority would rankle her.

"Abigail ..." Miranda began.

I put a finger up to signal I would be with her in a moment while I typed out the lyrics to a Duran Duran song. Finally, I sighed, minimized my document, and turned to her. She was pissed at being ignored. "Coffee, Miranda?" I did not apologize or acknowledge the wait.

Whatever she thought I was going to say, this was not it. "Yes, that would be nice. Thank you."

I nodded and walked over to Deveraux's in-room coffee bar. "One sugar and a splash of milk, correct?"

"Correct." I could feel her looking me over. "Where did you get the Dior knockoff?" she asked with a sniff.

Bitch. "It's not a knockoff. It's a vintage suit my mother owned." And I sent up thanks for Mom and I being the same size. "I am surprised you can't tell the difference."

"Of course, I can. I was surprised to see you in a real designer suit." I rolled my eyes but said nothing.

I set her coffee in front of her and sat behind Deveraux's desk—correction: my desk. "I can't think why you'd be surprised."

"You never cared about how you looked before."

"Now, you know that's not true. But there is quite a bit happening today. The suit felt appropriate." I took a breath. "I'm sure you've heard about Mason."

"Yes, it's terrible." I watched as she tried to eke out a tear and failed miserably. "I hope they find him soon."

"They won't, Miranda. You probably already suspect that."

"How could I?" Still playing innocent. "You certainly seem comfortable behind his desk."

"My desk, Miranda."

"Excuse me?"

"My desk. It's my desk now. And yes, I do happen to know Mason won't be coming back. Mason Deveraux is dead." The color drained from her face as she figured out how much shit she was in. "Ah, the penny has dropped."

"You little bitch!" She went for her purse and found it missing.

"Looking for this?" I asked, holding up the bag I had grabbed when I had set her coffee down. Jack had suggested that little move, suspecting she might go after phone or possibly a weapon. He'd been correct.

"Give me that!" she shrieked, flying out of her seat.

"Miranda Summers, shut the fuck up and sit the fuck down." I stood. "I don't want to have you put back in your seat, but I will."

"I'd like to see you try! Do you know who I am?"

"You mean besides my Uncle Evan's mistress?" She looked at me in shock. "Yes, I know about that. Now, sit. I am more than capable of forcing you to."

She sat heavily. "Abigail, you, of all people, should understand what it's like to be a woman in the business world!"

I laughed. "Miranda, you haven't worked a day in your life. You're on the board of a handful of companies. It's hardly a job." I snapped my fingers. "Oh, and to be clear, that ends today."

"What are you talking about?"

"All will be made clear soon. Our other guests should be here momentarily." That was the signal for Anderson to come in with Jennings. The office was still bugged, so he and Jack heard everything. "Now, drink your coffee and keep your mouth shut."

We waited another couple of minutes before the door opened, and Anderson walked in with Jack, and Soames and Keith frog-marched Jennings in. A woman I didn't recognize came in behind them. I assumed this was Anderson's sister, June. My eyes widened. She was Korean, like her brother, and utterly breathtaking with long, dark hair with blue highlights, a full mouth, cheekbones that could cut glass, and very tall. Had their father chosen his children based on their beauty?

I cleared my throat. "Ah, Marc Jennings." I looked at Miranda. "I believe you two are acquainted."

"You little bitch ..." He got nothing else out as Anderson grabbed him by his collar and pulled. "I suggest," he said in a soft voice that in no way masked the menace, "you choose your words with the utmost care." He pushed Jennings into the chair next to Miranda.

"Well, now that you both are here, let's have a little chat, shall we?" I folded my hands. "Jennings, as I've just informed Miranda, Deveraux will not be coming back. He's dead. And this little game of yours is at an end. You've played with my father's life and mine. You framed him for embezzlement, and once I got too close, you hatched a plan to kill me."

"It wasn't our idea!" Jennings shouted.

"If you continue to shout, I will be forced to ask Anderson to keep you quiet. I am certain you don't want that." Someone snorted, and I realized it had come from June. "Now, I know this wasn't your idea. It was my uncle's. And rest assured, he will be dealt with next."

"How do you mean?" Jennings asked.

"Oh, that's nothing for you to worry about," I said with a smile. I held up a thumb drive. "All the information needed to try and convict him and you is here. My father is scrupulous about his records. He discovered everything: the theft, the payouts, all of it." I turned to Miranda. "He even discovered your affair with my uncle. There's photographic proof here. And him, a married man. Such a shame."

"So, you're going to turn us in?" Miranda said.

"No," I said. "Neither of you will be going to jail."

"I don't understand!" Jennings was almost turning purple with rage.

"Yes, you do," said Anderson. "Marc Jennings, you are going to die."

Jennings jumped up and slammed his fists on the desk. "You little fucking slut! You had to go poking your nose in where it didn't belong. You think fucking a vampire is going to protect you from us? You're wrong!"

Anderson sighed, grabbed him, and threw him against the wall. "I shouldn't have let him go on, but I did want to see if he would hang himself. He's just as idiotic as Deveraux."

I shook my head. "I thought you weren't going to play with your food, Anderson." This time, June let out an outright laugh which helped. My knees were shaking badly, and I was glad I could use the desk for support. I knew what he was about to do, and I couldn't flinch. I needed Miranda as scared of me as she was of Anderson.

"I'm not, darling." He picked Jennings up and held him against the wall, hand wrapped around his neck, cutting off his air supply. "Marc Jennings, I find you guilty. You are sentenced to death." With that, Anderson pulled him off the wall and snapped his neck.

I didn't move. I didn't blink. I watched it happen. The body dropped to the floor. *Later. I'll deal with it later.* I looked at Miranda. "And now, for you."

Miranda started to cry actual tears. "How could you watch that happen? You're as much a monster as he is."

I shook my head. "I am not the monster. Neither is he." I gestured to Anderson.

"And you are no longer welcome in my city," Anderson said as his sister came forward. "This is my sister, June. You'll be going with her."

"I ... I don't understand. Going where?"

"Oh, it hardly matters," June answered. Oh, fuck me, that voice of hers ... It was lyrical. "You won't be seeing much of the world anymore."

"For how long?" Miranda asked.

"The rest of your life, dear. I am sure I can find some use for you." She looked over Miranda thoroughly. "Hopefully," she sneered.

"I have to pack or something. I don't ... I don't know." She looked lost. The fight had left her. I almost felt bad for her. Almost.

June laughed. "Pack? Oh no, my dear. You will wear the clothes I provide. Your life as Miranda Summers ends today. You will never see your friends or family again, I am afraid. Though, I am given to understand you aren't blessed with an abundance of either." She lifted Miranda out of her chair. "But first, apologize to Ms. Eastman."

"I apologize, Abigail. I am sorry for all of it." She tried to act contrite, but it was optics. She was trying to save her own ass.

I walked around the desk and stood in front of her. "I don't forgive you." Then I pulled back and slammed my fist into her face.

June laughed again, and Anderson smiled. Jack, Soames, and Keith looked shocked.

"Delightful." June looked at Miranda. "That apology was appalling. That is something we will need to work on. Sincere contrition." June then turned to Soames and Keith. "Can you please deliver her to my car? My people are waiting."

They nodded and led Miranda out. June put out her hand. "June Jeon. I quite like your style."

"Abigail Eastman. I like yours as well."

"You're going to need to bring her to meet *abeoji*, you know?" She looked at Anderson. "He's going to adore her."

"I know," Anderson said, coming over, putting his arm around me, and pulling me close.

"I am glad you have finally found someone, *hyeongje*. I shall speak with you soon."

"Thank you, *jamae*. It was good to see you."

She nodded and left the room.

"I must say, Abigail," Jack began, "you were amazing."

"You were indeed," Anderson agreed.

I blushed a little. "Thank you." I looked over at Jennings. "I don't feel anything. Shouldn't I?" I looked at the two men.

Anderson looked at Jennings. "Right now, you're likely still processing it all. You may have a lot of adrenaline from what's happening, though your heartbeat is steady. Add to the fact this person caused you a lot of pain where it concerns your father. You not feeling anything is not unreasonable."

I nodded. "So, this might hit me later, is what you're saying."

"That's how it was with me," Jack said. "I was still a young man, and it was difficult." Anderson and I looked at him in surprise but didn't say anything.

Soames and Keith came back in. "Handoff accomplished," said Soames.

"She cried like a baby," Keith put in. "I took a video."

"You did not!" I exclaimed.

"He most certainly did," Soames replied. "I asked him to." She shrugged. "Women like that make me itchy."

"Part of me wants to see it, but the other part thinks I am awful to want to."

"She called you all kinds of horrible names if that helps," said Soames. "Said a lot of shit about your mom too."

"Oh, really? Send it to me then."

"If we're done with that, please move Jennings' body back to his home. Place him at the bottom of the stairs."

"Make it look like he fell, you mean?" Keith asked.

"I do mean that."

"How will you get him past everyone in the office?"

"Abigail, I had the floor cleared as soon as Miranda entered your office. Once Jennings is out, we'll allow them back onto the floor."

I leaned up and kissed his cheek. "So smart," I said. "What now?"

"Your uncle. If you're up for it."

"I am. I want this to be done." I stopped and took a deep breath. "Has it only been a little over a week?"

"It has," Anderson said. He gave me a strange, almost sad look. I'd have to ask him about it later when we were alone. "But what a week."

I nodded. "Okay, let's get this done."

ANDERSON

I held Abigail's hand on the way to her uncle's office. We were both quiet, lost in our thoughts. Jack was in the front seat, busily keeping all the balls moving for us. Despite her declarations yesterday, I was worried my little flower would discover she didn't love me once this was over and things had calmed down. I was worried she didn't want to be tied to a vampire any longer.

This was not a feeling I enjoyed. I would never hold her against her will, but it would hurt. And the fact that it would was upsetting to me. It had been many, many years since I had felt something besides a superficial interest in a woman. Or much of anything if I was being honest with myself. For all my big talk about control and power, my emotional well-being hinged on the woman next to me.

It both humbled me and pissed me off.

"We're here," Jack said, breaking into my thoughts.

"Okay," said Abbie. "Would you mind waiting outside the car for a moment? I want to speak to Anderson."

"I don't think now is the time ..." I began, slightly panicked.

"Now is the time. Uncle Evan is not going anywhere, and we need to talk."

"We'll be right outside." Jack and the driver got out of the car.

Abbie turned to look at me. "What's wrong?"

"Nothing is wrong, Abigail."

"Liar," she said softly. "I saw your face earlier. Now you're holding my hand like it's a lifeline. What's up? Are you planning on dumping me when this is over?"

I gave her a startled look. "No! What? Why would you think that?"

"Then why are you acting so weird?"

I raked my hand through my hair. "I am concerned that once the dust settles, you may discover you aren't in love with me." Being vulnerable is bullshit, frankly. I had never felt so exposed. This was awful.

"So, what you're saying is you don't think I know my own mind and heart well enough to figure out whether I am really in love or high on the fumes of corporate corruption?"

"I did not say that ... precisely."

"No, you said precisely that. So, when I told you I'd always love you, I was lost in the moment of visiting my father in prison?" She was glaring at me. "You are stuck with me. I am well aware we've been together for a minute. I am also cognizant of the fact that it's completely ridiculous to be in love. Yet here we sit, in love with one another. I see you, Anderson Jeon. And you see me. You won't get rid of me that easily."

I pulled her into my arms and held her. "Fuck, Abbie. I'm sorry."

"Good. You should be, you asshole. Your sister likes me, so I am in. I'm staying."

"I am not an easy person to love," I said.

"Oh, fuck off! Yes, you are." She pulled back. "At least, so far." She smiled at me, and it was like the sun breaking through the clouds.

"Jae-Seong," I said suddenly.

Her eyes widened. "Is that the name you were born with?"

I nodded. "Our given names are kept in the family. It is the way my father wishes it."

"Why the name Anderson?"

"Many years ago, I had a friend who's last name was that. He was human, and once he passed, I changed it to honor him."

"That is so sweet. You honor me by trusting me with your given name," she said quietly, giving me a soft kiss.

"It is I who is honored by your love."

"So, no more of this nonsense then?"

"No more," I replied.

"Good! Now, let's go kick some ass."

"As you wish, little flower."

***

She was brilliant when we got upstairs. She barged right in like she owned the place.

"Is Mr. Woodman in his office?" she asked his assistant as she breezed past her desk.

"Oh, Miss ... Miss, he's busy!"

"Oh, I'm *family*. I am sure he has time for me."

"Oh, no, please don't. He'll be angry," the assistant pleaded.

Abbie paused, her hand on the doorknob. "What's your name, dear?"

"Marcy," came the answer.

"Marcy, you won't need to worry about him after today."

She looked at us. "Really?"

"Yes, really," I replied. "It will be a bit bumpy for a while. But Woodman will be gone." I looked around. "Very soon, the police are going to show up. Please send them in."

She nodded and returned to her seat as Abbie opened the office door. "Uncle Evan! I've come to visit."

We stepped inside, and Evan stood behind his desk, staring at us. There were two other people in his office. "Leave," I told them. They scurried out quickly.

"This is outrageous!" Evan Woodman was a man who kept himself up, appearance-wise. He was good-looking. I could see how Miranda Summers could be attracted to him. Dark hair, good build, great suits. But his eyes were cold.

"Is it, though? This can't be completely unexpected," I said. "Surely Miranda or Jennings have kept you updated."

"Who?" he asked. "I don't think I know them."

"You are a terrible liar, Uncle." Abbie stared at him. He stared back, but she kept eye contact. He looked away first.

I held up the thumb drive. "It's all here, all the proof we need to free Jacob Eastman and put you in prison."

"And I suppose the others will join me there?" Woodman smirked.

"Hardly," I replied. "Jennings and Deveraux are quite dead, and Summers is now in the care of my sister, June." I had the pleasure of him paling under that tan of his.

"No death for me, then?"

"Abigail has requested I not kill you."

He looked at her. "So, you have compassion for me then?"

"Not at all," she replied. "I want to watch you suffer. I want to watch as you lose everything and your entire world comes crashing down around you. I want to watch what you did to my father be done to you."

He stared at her, and then his legs gave out. He slumped into his chair. "You have no idea what it's like to watch your company crumble around you. The lengths you'll go to ensure your legacy is secure."

Abbie marched over and slammed her fists on the table. "You narcissistic prick! I watched my mother reach out to you and your parents time and time again, only to be rebuffed, ignored, and asked to leave her own mother's funeral. Then, you have the blue-blooded balls to ask my father to help you out of your predicament. A predicament you wouldn't be in if you weren't so shit at your job."

"Abigail, you must see ..."

"I don't see anything but a man who concocted a plot to save his own skin while sacrificing his niece in the process. I almost feel sorry for Miranda. God knows what you told her."

"You have no proof."

"Incorrect," I said. "We have photographic evidence that was provided to your wife as of about three minutes ago. Chances are, she's already on the phone with a divorce attorney."

"How dare you!"

I went over to him and leaned down, boxing him in. "No. How dare you! You have used and betrayed people. All for what? To keep your image intact? Everyone knows your father was disappointed in you. But it's what he deserved, and one day, you will rot in hell with him.

"What's really offensive is how sloppy all of this was. It wasn't hard to find. You are the most incompetent group of people. This was destined to fail. But maybe you were too focused on a personal vendetta all along." Abigail smirked at him.

"I have connections. I will be out in no time."

"No, you won't. This is my city. I'm in charge. You are going to jail. And since you saw fit to make sure Jacob Eastman went to a medium-security prison, you'll be going to be a maximum. It's the least I can do."

Someone knocked, and Marcy poked her head in. "Police are here," she said gleefully.

"Send them in," I said.

A handful of uniformed cops and two plainclothes detectives came in. "Mr. Jeon?" One said. "You have something for us?"

"Yes, Pete. Thank you for coming." I handed him a copy of the thumb drive. "On this drive is everything needed to exonerate Jacob Eastman and convict Evan Woodman of conspiracy to frame Mr. Eastman."

"Well, you've been busy. Interestingly, we just got a call that Marc Jennings was found dead this morning. Broken neck. Poor bastard fell down the stairs."

"What a pity."

"Ain't it just? Deveraux is still missing. Is Miranda Summers also missing?"

"Highly likely," I replied blandly. "She visited Ms. Eastman this morning but had to be escorted out of the building by security."

"Will I find footage?"

"Highly unlikely," I said.

"Thought as much." He turned to Woodman. "Alright, Woodman, on your feet!"

"This is an outrage!" Woodman yelled.

"Nope, this is an arrest," replied my detective friend.

It took time to get everything sorted out, but eventually, Woodman was led out in handcuffs and to thunderous applause. He was not well-liked. We took another hour to explain everything to the CFO, who had no clue what was going on. That was worrisome.

"What's going to happen to the company?" he asked.

"We're going to see what his wife wants to do. It's still family-owned, and she's his only family. My guess is she'll sell it." I would offer to buy it and decide what became of it while caring for the employees. "For now, business as usual."

We had almost escaped when Woodman's wife flew in like a bat out of hell. That took another couple of hours. She had a keen mind. She wanted to take it slow but said she'd contact me if she wanted to sell.

Back at Abbie's, I relaxed, watching her cook. "We can go out," I said. "Or get something delivered."

"Cooking relaxes me. So, does lasagna." She drank some wine. "I'm out of ground beef, so it's going to be veggie lasagna. There will be a lot of cheese though."

"For someone who says their favorite meal is a burger, we have a lot of pasta," I said.

Abbie burst out laughing. "Holy shit! You're right. Well, who doesn't love carbs?"

"How are you feeling?"

"Good. Weird but good. My aunt is a cool customer. It was odd. I would be breathing fire if I was her."

"Well, it's obvious they hated each other. And I would never cheat, so need to worry there." I picked up a piece of bread and chewed on it. "There are a lot of loose ends to work out still. I want to make sure we take care of people. Woodman's employees should not be collateral damage."

"Big scary vampire taking care of the people," I joked.

"Abigail, I killed someone in front of you today. I am fairly concerned it's not bothering you now that we've all calmed down, and you aren't processing it appropriately."

"Anderson, I have a therapist. I emailed her earlier, and as luck would have it, she specializes in human-vampire relationships. Therefore, this is something I can and will work through with her. It won't change my mind, though. You're stuck with me. I love you too much."

"And you love the orgasms I give you," I said, relief flooding me. I wasn't going to lose her.

"I mean, true. I am curious what you and I look like without having to foil bad guys."

"Me too," I replied. "But I admit I often do have people to foil."

"Well, it will never be boring." She looked at the pot. "The sauce needs to simmer. Come with me." She led me into the bedroom. She had changed when we'd gotten back and was wearing a short dress. "I need you naked." She unbuttoned my shirt as I unbuckled my belt and slid my pants off.

"Are you compartmentalizing with sex right now?" I asked.

"Yes, I am."

"Works for me, little flower."

She slid my shirt off and stopped. The bare place over my heart wasn't bare any longer. There was a tattoo there now, and it was her. She traced the outline, barely able to speak. "When did you do this?" she asked quietly.

"Last night, when I went back to my place. Vampires don't need healing time for tattoos."

"It's me," she said. "You got a tattoo of me."

"Of course, it is. Who else would I put over my heart? My heart does not beat often, but when it does, it beats only for you."

She rested her head against my chest, her hand still over my heart. I put my hand over hers. "I can see why you'd worry about me changing my mind now," she said, weakly.

"Wouldn't matter. I'd never regret placing you over my heart."

"You fucker," she said.

I chuckled. "I know."

She pulled back and smiled at me "Lay on the bed." I did as she asked. She opened her drawer and got a toy out, flicking it on. She moved it over her breasts while looking at me. "Take yourself in hand, Anderson. I want to watch you stroke yourself."

Fuck! This woman. I took my cock and stroked slowly as she used the toy on her breasts. She groaned and moved the toy until it was against her clit.

"Pinch your nipples for me, baby."

"Yes, Anderson." She pinched her nipples hard as she worked the toy around her clit.

"God, baby, I can see how wet you are. Do you want to come there or on my cock?"

"On your cock," she said. "I want to ride you."

"Then come over here."

She turned the toy off and crawled onto the bed, straddling me. She positioned herself right over me. I put my hands on her hips and pushed her onto my cock. We both moaned.

"Fuck me, little flower."

She moved slowly at first. I let her set the rhythm. She rolled a nipple between her fingers as I sucked on the other. My fangs dropped and scraped over her nipple. She bucked against me, and I repeated it on the other nipple.

"Anderson!" She cried. "Fuck, do that again with your fangs. It feels amazing."

I ran my fangs along her clavicle, stopping to suck the skin every so often. I bit her gently, not enough to drink, but enough to mark her. She groaned and clutched my shoulders, riding me faster now.

"So fucking beautiful," I breathed. "Look at you. Look at my marks on you."

"Anderson, please. More."

"More what, little flower?"

"Just more."

I sucked on her neck as I thrust into her and reached for her clit. I took it between two fingers as I pumped harder. She met each stroke with her own. "Come on, baby. Come on my cock now like a good girl."

"No, not a good girl."

"No? My filthy little angel, then. Is that what you are right now?" I pinched her clit, and she bucked as we sped up, bodies slapping together, breathing uneven.

"Yes, yes!"

"My filthy angel, time to come for me then. Come on my cock." She fused her mouth to mine, and we rocked together. She exploded, and I closed my eyes and exploded with her.

Later that night, after dinner and another fuck in the kitchen, she slept beside me. I rolled over onto my side, and she followed.

"Everything okay?" I asked.

"Yes," she said sleepily. "I thought you might like to be the little spoon for once."

"You know," I said with wonder in my voice. "I do like it. I like it very much."

JACK

One month later

I looked around the room and smiled to myself. Cam was in the corner speaking with Lacey and her husband. Our eyes met. She smiled softly at me. We were taking things slow. Anderson and Abbie had been like a freight train, which freaked us out a little, so we were taking our time. It didn't matter, though. She was it for me. I was unsure what she saw in me, sweet as she was. But I wasn't going to question it too deeply.

The ladies' friendship with Bree had officially ended. Bree's father found out about her husband's cheating and put his foot down. You didn't cheat on his daughter. He'd transferred his son-in-law to the main office across the country, so he could keep an eye on him. Bree packed up and moved back home without a word to the women she'd been friends with since college.

Abbie was talking to Mel and my sister. Yes, Cam convinced me to start calling her Abbie. Abbie been a godsend to my sister, and they'd become fast friends.

Anderson was deep in conversation with Jacob and another man who was the CFO of Evan Woodman's old company. Woodman's ex-wife wanted to run the company and asked for Anderson's help. According to him, she was doing a better job than Evan had. She had also taken her brother in hand after Anderson had told her of his involvement. That man did not go to the bathroom without his sister's okay at this point.

It had taken, much to Anderson's ire, another week to secure Jacob's release. This gave Abbie time to find him an apartment. Coincidentally, one opened in her building, four floors up and on the opposite side from Abbie's place. She'd be close to her dad, but they'd be able to maintain their privacy.

It hadn't even taken as much money as Anderson expected for that apartment to become available. I am pretty sure Abbie suspected, but she didn't let on.

Jennings' death was ruled an accident. We released a story that Deveraux and Summers had gone on the run together. Eventually, we'd release a story that they'd died together, too.

Miranda Summers, surprisingly, had taken to being under June's thumb, at least to hear June tell it. And Anderson was grateful not to have that death on his conscience.

He killed with ease when necessary, but he'd prefer not to. It was an old-fashioned notion. For me, the bad guy could be a bad lady just as easily.

I heard Cam laugh and stopped to watch her. Christ, she was breathtaking.

All in all, though, things were in order for the moment, and I liked that. Work to be done still, but it was all progressing.

My phone pinged, and I looked at it and smiled. I sidled over to Anderson. "Woodman's trial date is set. Should be quick."

"Good," said Anderson. "But now go have fun."

I nodded as he walked over to Abbie and put his arms around her from behind. "If you told me when she was ten that she'd be in love with a vampire who was equally over the moon for her, I'd have thought you were crazy. But they fit."

I looked at Jacob Eastman. He was starting to put some weight on again, thanks to Abbie's cooking, and he looked relaxed. "They do fit."

"So do you and Cam." He cleared his throat. "Son, you should know, I knew your father."

I stiffened. "Oh?"

"Yes. Went to school with him. Always was a mean son of a bitch. None of that was your fault. You were still just a kid yourself."

I said nothing, but nodded slightly.

He squeezed my shoulder. "Cam is looking at you, worried. Go talk to her."

"Sir?" I managed to croak out.

"It's not my story to tell, and I won't. You can count on me." He nudged me. "Now, go to talk to your lady," he said as he wandered off.

I stood still for a few moments. Jacob Eastman was a good man. Shit, I wish he'd been my father. He had just wanted me to know that I was seen. Or at least the boy I had been was seen. I took a deep breath, and then let it go.

It was a nice party, as far as parties go. But it was hard not to be on my guard all the time. It was a lifelong habit.

I walked toward Cam. Work could wait. Tonight was a celebration, and for once, I would relax and enjoy myself.

All was well.

Acknowledgements

Marked by the Vampire came to me in a dream. Literally. I had this dream about a fully tatted, Korean vampire who was sexy as hell, and I had to write him. It's possible I had been watching too many Korean dramas on Netflix. But, can you blame me? Anyway, it's Anderson's fault that you don't have *Demon's Heart* in your hands at this point, but hopefully you're not too mad at him. And *Demon's Heart* is coming. I promise.

Thanks to my breasties (you know, besties but with...breasts. You get it), for their unwavering love and support. Get you a group of friends where you can take turns being the one who has their shit together, and the one who is a spicy disaster.

Thanks to my beta readers; Erin, Heather, and Kristin. The feedback as always, makes the book better, and if they're excited about something – I know I am on the right track.

Thank you to my editor Kyleigh who once again put me on the right path. Any errors you see are mine.

And thanks to my proofreader extraordinaire, Sheri Williams. Not only is she an awesome friend, she is a wonderul proofreader. And she will make the book better with her comments and suggestions. Sheri, I swear that I really do like contractions. Sheri was also the person that confirmed that I needed to write this story. Any further errors you see are mine, and mine alone. She tried to warn me, after all. Also, go read Sheri's books, because she is an amazing writer.

Finally, thank you, the reader. For reading and hopefully enjoying this book. And thank you for supporting indie authors. Without you all, we writers would just be sitting in dark rooms, banging away on a keyboard with no one to read our work. I mean, we do that, but at least we have people who read our books. If you enjoyed this book, or any of my books, please consider reviewing or rating it on Amazon. This helps us indies out immensely.

And in case you're wondering; this gang will be back with at least 2 more books.

About the Author

Lori-Anne Cohen is an urban fantasy and paranormal romance author, living and working in Massachusetts. She is a cat mom, sometimes actress, and she never uses a level when hanging things on the wall as she likes to live dangerously.

Want to know where to find me, or about my other titles? See the QR code below.

Titles by Lori-Anne Cohen

Demons of Paris Series
Demon's Consort
Demon's Guardian
Demon's Holiday
Demon's Heart – Coming 2025

Vampire's Kiss Series
Vampire's Kiss
Vampire's Trouble – Coming 2025/2026

Marked by the Vampire

Riding the Dragon

www.ingramcontent.com/pod-product-compliance
Lightning Source LLC
Chambersburg PA
CBHW051706180726
48283CB00004B/1230
* 9 7 8 1 7 3 7 0 8 3 8 7 0 *